Choose your Lane to love!

I0659825

A Few Good Fish

"…this book is the perfect combination of romance and suspense, and pulls together the storylines that have been building up over the past two books just perfectly."

—Joyfully Jay

A Fool and His Manny

"Reading this novel is like being enveloped in large, welcoming mommy arms or walking in the door home and getting the welcome you always dreamed about from the family you always wanted."

—Scattered Thoughts and Rogue Words

Stand by Your Manny

"*Stand by Your Manny* is a wonderful tale of young love, first kisses and touches, and shows why there's really no one better at writing families of all kinds than Amy Lane."

—Diverse Reader

By Amy Lane

Published by DREAMSPINNER PRESS
www.dreamspinnerpress.com

By AMY LANE

KEEPING PROMISE ROCK
Keeping Promise Rock • Making
Promises
Living Promises • Forever
Promised

JOHNNIES
Chase in Shadow • Dex in Blue
Ethan in Gold • Black John
Bobby Green
Super Sock Man

GRANBY KNITTING
The Winter Courtship Rituals of
Fur-Bearing Critters
How to Raise an Honest Rabbit •
Knitter in His Natural Habitat
Blackbird Knitting in a Bunny's
Lair
The Granby Knitting Menagerie
Anthology

TALKER
Talker • Talker's Redemption •
Talker's Graduation
The Talker Collection Anthology

WINTER BALL
Winter Ball • Summer Lessons

Published by Harmony Ink Press
BITTER MOON SAGA
Triane's Son Rising • Triane's Son
Learning
Triane's Son Fighting • Triane's
Son Reigning

Published by DREAMSPINNER PRESS
www.dreamspinnerpress.com

Regret Me Not

Amy Lane

DREAMSPINNER
PRESS

Published by

DREAMSPINNER PRESS

5032 Capital Circle SW, Suite 2, PMB# 279, Tallahassee, FL 32305-7886 USA
www.dreamspinnerpress.com

This is a work of fiction. Names, characters, places, and incidents either are the product of author imagination or are used fictitiously, and any resemblance to actual persons, living or dead, business establishments, events, or locales is entirely coincidental.

Regret Me Not
© 2017, 2019 Amy Lane.

Cover Art
© 2019 Reese Dante.
http://www.reesedante.com
Cover content is for illustrative purposes only and any person depicted on the cover is a model.

All rights reserved. This book is licensed to the original purchaser only. Duplication or distribution via any means is illegal and a violation of international copyright law, subject to criminal prosecution and upon conviction, fines, and/or imprisonment. Any eBook format cannot be legally loaned or given to others. No part of this book may be reproduced or transmitted in any form or by any means, electronic or mechanical, including photocopying, recording, or by any information storage and retrieval system, without the written permission of the Publisher, except where permitted by law. To request permission and all other inquiries, contact Dreamspinner Press, 5032 Capital Circle SW, Suite 2, PMB# 279, Tallahassee, FL 32305-7886, USA, or www.dreamspinnerpress.com.

Trade Paperback ISBN: 978-1-64080-970-3
Digital ISBN: 978-1-63533-995-6
Library of Congress Control Number: 2018952498
Trade Paperback published January 2019
Digital eBook published December 2017
v. 1.0

Printed in the United States of America
∞
This paper meets the requirements of
ANSI/NISO Z39.48-1992 (Permanence of Paper).

Mate, for happy endings even though he's becoming the "get off my lawn" guy. Mary, for cheerleading—this is your perfect book, hon. I always love writing those for you. Kids, for putting up with me and hugs every night anyway. And Karen, for letting me sleep in your condo (when I was supposed to be working) and booking me my first massage and, generally, hospitality and friendship and inspiration.

THE MORNING AFTER....

THE EVER-PRESENT shush of the sea echoed in his ears. Even before he was awake, Pierce Atwater knew that sound had haunted him in his dreams.

He yawned and stretched, the familiar aches of healing injuries pulling at his skin and muscles and the unfamiliar ache in his backside waking him up fully. Oh, hey. It had been a while since that happened.

With a heave, Pierce sat up entirely, getting his bearings. The beach house he'd lived in since Thanksgiving glowed as bright and gold as he remembered—too beautiful. Almost pristine.

His body, on the other hand—that felt well-used.

He turned and looked at the bed he'd just vacated, noting that it was rumpled and sex stained; lovemaking and sweat permeated the room.

Oh wow. Oh damn. What had he done?

A piece of paper—the ripped-off corner of a brown grocery bag—caught his attention on the other pillow of the king-sized bed.

Please don't leave without saying goodbye—

—H

Pierce stared at the note, only marginally prepared for the giant ache that bloomed in his chest.

Aw, Hal—you deserve so very much more.

He looked around the room again, eyes falling on the clock radio. He was supposed to leave in an hour—he'd told his sister specifically that he'd be in Orlando by lunch so he could bake cookies with her kids.

He looked at the note again and tried hard to breathe.

THE MONTH BEFORE

"SO YOU have the Lyft app, right?"

"Yeah, Sasha—don't worry about me, okay?" Pierce regarded his younger sister fondly. She was made to be a mother—even if she came into being one a little young.

Sasha bit her lip, trying not to argue. She'd been such a sweet kid growing up—never saying boo to either of their rather domineering parents. She'd gotten pregnant right out of high school, and even though Marshall had stepped up and married her and they'd both managed to get their degrees, their parents... well, they'd never let Sasha live down what a disappointment she'd been. Or—their words—what a slut either.

Pierce had hated them long before Sasha got pregnant, but the way they'd tried to destroy her for a simple human failing had sort of sealed the deal.

But parenthood had made Sasha—and Marshall—a great deal stronger than they'd been as feckless teenagers, and while Sasha wouldn't *argue* with her beloved older brother, she would *discuss* things she disagreed with.

"Pierce, you almost died," she said quietly, her thin face suddenly lost in the pallor of anxiety and the cloud of fine dark hair she could never keep back in a ponytail. "I mean... I refuse to see Mom and Dad over the holidays because they're just... just...."

"Awful," he supplied with feeling. Yeah. He'd resolved not to put up with awful anymore.

"Toxic," she agreed, leaning back against her aging SUV. Darius and Abigail were sleeping in the back seat after playing out in the surf under Pierce's supervision while Marshall and Sasha moved Pierce into the condo. Pierce had worried—he couldn't move very well without the cane these days, and what did he know about kids and water?

But mostly what they'd wanted to do was run away from the waves and collect shells, and the one time Abigail had been knocked on her ass into the surf, Pierce had bent down and picked her up by the hand before the pain even registered.

The move had hurt—but it had given him some hope. His doctors kept assuring him that he could get most of his mobility back if he kept active and remembered his aqua regimen. Picking Abigail up and reassuring her that Uncle Pierce wouldn't let her drown gave him some confidence that his body might someday be back up to par. And the condo had a pool, which was why he'd taken his best friend Derrick's offer to let him use it over the winter months while Pierce got his life together. Pierce was definitely in a position to follow his doctor's advice.

So now, looking at his sister and thinking about how much self-assurance she'd had to grow to push a little into Pierce's state of mind, he couldn't be mad at her.

And he had to be honest.

"I'll be grumpy and pissed off and bitter," he said, letting his mouth twist into a scowl of disdain for the land of the living. He'd been fighting it off since Sasha picked him up at the airport. "It's a good thing you made me get the car app, because seriously, I may have let myself starve to death. As it is, the groceries are going to keep me going for a good long time."

Sasha's eyes grew big and bright, and he took her hand and squeezed.

"Don't worry, sweetie. None of it is your fault. You would have let me stay at your place forever, and I was getting in your way. This is good. I'll hang out here, find a little peace, and when I go back to Orlando, I'll be up for getting my own apartment and getting out of your hair, okay?"

"I'd never kick you out, Pierce," she said miserably. "You know that." She wiped the back of her hand across her big brown eyes. "You just… you got out of the hospital and—"

"And I was an awful fucking bastard," he said with feeling. *Oh God.* The defining moment for calling up Derrick to take him up on his offer was when he'd heard his father's words coming out of his mouth, telling his sister she was useless because she couldn't help him off the couch without pain. "Sasha, you deserve better than me. You deserve better, period. I'm not going to hang around you and get in your way again until I'm decent company for human beings, okay?"

Sasha shook her head, still crying. "You were in pain," she whispered. "And you were sorry right after. And you've done so much for me, Pierce. I can forgive you for being mean once when you did so much for me...."

He remembered the night she'd shown up at his apartment, in tears, practically hysterical, because she'd told the parents about an impending Darius and had been read the riot act about what a fuckup she was.

He'd taken her in—let her stay with him for a couple of months until she and Marshall scraped up enough money for rent and a car. She'd gotten a job, and Pierce had paid her tuition as she made her way through school. She had a career now—one she could work from home as a developmental editor of a small press. Marshall had his degree in software engineering, and together they made a good living—good enough to afford a guest bedroom and to put Pierce up for a month after the accident.

Pierce squeezed her hand now. "You listen to me," he said gruffly. "You don't owe me a thing. You're the only family I want to see—pretty much ever. So just let me work shit out in my own head, and I'll come back for Christmas a whole new man, okay?"

"I like the one you are right now!" she said staunchly, and then she threw herself in his arms and held on tight. "Love you, big brother," she whispered, and Marshall stood behind her, guiding her away.

"Love you too," he said belatedly, and Marshall turned and shook his hand firmly.

"Come back when you promised, okay?" Marshall was just as slight as Sasha—two small, mild-mannered people getting along in a bright, brash world. Pierce had always fancied himself their champion knight—he couldn't be that as he was.

He had to make himself better.

"Christmas Eve," Pierce vowed. "Don't worry, Marshall. Nobody likes being alone on Christmas."

Marshall shrugged. "We wouldn't be alone, Pierce. We just don't want you to be."

With that, the guy Pierce and Sasha's parents had driven off their property with a baseball bat guided a disconsolate Sasha into the old vehicle and piloted it away.

As soon as they'd left the parking lot, Pierce allowed his shoulders to sag and dragged his sorry ass to the back door of the condo.

He crawled into bed and stayed there until he absolutely had to get up and pee the next morning.

STAYING IN bed for sixteen hours had consequences—he almost didn't make it to the bathroom, he was so sore. After he'd taken care of business and washed down a granola bar, he realized he was going to have to be serious about that pool thing, or he really could end up curling into a ball and dying in a beach condo in Florida.

For a moment he contemplated it—he'd always been the kind of guy to consider all the angles—but eventually he decided he wouldn't go quickly enough and managed a pair of board shorts and a T-shirt. As he walked through the tiled hall of the condo, he realized the tile was going to destroy his body almost as quickly as the inactivity, and made a mental note to buy some rubber mats at the very least, so he'd have some padding for his joints. Derrick had said to make himself at home—ergonomic home decorating was a go!

Just as soon as he got into the... ahhh... pool.

Heated, of course, and a perfect counterpoint to a cool day in the high fifties/low sixties. He'd set his phone on a lounge chair, playing something disgustingly upbeat and perky, and went about doing the exercises he and his physical therapist had worked on.

Actual physical motor activity really did have magical properties— it must have. He was working up a head of steam, the resistance and buoyancy of the water supporting his body as he used active stretching techniques, when a voice cut into his workout Zen.

"If you don't straighten your back, you'll be in a world of hurt!"

Crap. Whoever that was, he was right.

Pierce adjusted his form and then looked over his right shoulder, from whence the voice—deep and sharp and young—had issued.

"Thanks," he said briefly, taking in the sprawled form of what looked to be a teenager wearing board shorts, a leopard-print bathrobe, and giant aviator sunglasses, lounging in one of the chaises. Dark hair, faintly sun streaked, was cut almost Boy Scout short around an adorable frat boy face. His hands were sort of a mess, loosely wrapped in gauze, but other than that, he was as untouched as a virgin's dreams.

"Dude, what in the hell are you listening to? This shit." The boy shuddered. "I'm saying. I bet you could work up a sweat if you had decent music."

"It's a mix," Pierce said weakly, feeling old and slow. "I just hit an easy button, you kn—"

"I'll get you a better sound," the kid said, picking up the phone. "What's your password?"

Pierce gave it to him and then stopped dead in the water and almost drowned. He was in the deep end, and he had to work to stay afloat and—

"Don't spaz," the kid said on a note of deep disgust. "My phone's in the condo, and I could give a shit about your passwords. Jesus, if I was a hacker genius, I'd be someplace warm, you think?"

Pierce took a deep breath, and suddenly Katy Perry came blaring out of his phone. Well, okay, so everybody had heard this song; it did make him want to work harder. Pierce was calling it a win.

"Thanks," he said again, panting now because he was moving faster.

The kid shrugged. "Don't worry about it. You gonna be here tomorrow?"

"Yeah, but—"

"Same time?"

"Yeah." 'Cause why not. Nothing better to do, right? No job, no wife, no life?

"Good. I'll see you here with better music. Now stop doing that water walk thing and do a mountain climber—come on—I know you can."

Pierce glared at him—and switched the move.

"There you go. Now follow my pace. You can go faster." The kid started clapping, and Pierce struggled to keep up.

"I can't… do… that…," he gasped. He expected attitude back, because the kid had given him nothing but, and he was surprised when the clapping slowed.

"Sorry. You just look younger than this pace."

Pierce had his back to the kid, but he had the sensation of a thorough visual once-over. He adjusted to the new pace and found his wind again. "Car accident," he managed, trying not to be offended.

"Aw… aw hell. I'm sorry. I'm being an ass. I should just leave you to your workout."

"No," Pierce called out, stopping to tread water and cool down enough to talk. "Sorry—just… I was getting a workout. I suck doing this alone." He kept his arms and legs moving and found the kid on the side of the pool again—he'd moved from where Pierce had first spotted him to stand right in front of the line Pierce was using to go back and forth.

"Yeah, well, being alone sort of sucks on all fronts," the kid said philosophically. "I'll try not to be an ass if you try to do a hard workout, how's that?"

Pierce found himself nodding, even though he'd only come out to the pool out of what he deemed necessity. "Deal," he panted.

"Okay, now back to mountain climbers. I'll set the pace, and if it's too fast, cry uncle."

"Groovy," Pierce breathed, positioning himself to go. "Now shoot."

The kid put him through a decently difficult workout, adjusting for the things Pierce couldn't do yet and pushing him hard in the stuff he could. After forty-five minutes, Pierce was starting to cramp up, though, and the kid had him stretch out.

Good stuff, really—the blue freedom of the water, the structure of the workout, and the congeniality of dealing with another human being without bitterness or backstory served as sort of a purge—some of the self-pity Pierce had wallowed in for the past sixteen hours was rinsed away.

But not all of it.

He was getting out of the pool when the damage in his calf and thigh screamed protest, and he groaned and grabbed on to the rail. The kid was right there, though, stepping into the water regardless of his pricey flip-flops and the hem of his leopard-print bathrobe.

"Uh-oh—overdid it. C'mon, let me help you to the hot tub. I'll give you a rubdown, okay?"

"No," Pierce grunted, suddenly aware of this kid. Lean and narrow but defined practically by muscle group, his body was a work of art, and Pierce didn't even know if he was of age. And even if he was of age, he was too damned young for Pierce.

"No hot tub?" the kid asked sharply. "Or no gay guy touching you?"

Pierce's face heated. "No hot teenager touching me?" he mumbled, limping toward the steamy goodness of the little spa and trying not to lean too much into the kid's strong arms.

The youngster's throaty chuckle didn't reassure him in the least. "I'm twenty-three, old man, so cool your jets. Besides, I'm"—his voice dropped sadly, and the suddenly vulnerable look on his frat boy face made him look even younger—"well, I'd like to become a massage therapist, but I've only got half the coursework and hours done. Seriously, though, I'm halfway a professional, and I'm pretty good, so maybe let me work out the cramp in your leg?" He smiled winningly and used his free hand to lift his shades so he could bat a pair of admittedly limpid and arresting amber-brown eyes. "After all, I did work you over pretty hard."

Pierce rolled his eyes at the double entendre, but as he reached for the rail of the hot tub, he had to concede that having his leg worked on would make the whole working-out thing feel like less of a mistake.

"Yeah, sure," he muttered, taking the steps creakily one at a time. "Sure, you can squeeze my muscles till I scream."

The kid chuckled again, inviting Pierce in on the laugh. "So you're happy to let me rub one out on you?"

Pierce groaned. "God, kid, I can hardly walk. No sex jokes until I can make it out of the pool without collapsing."

"So there can be sex jokes. Eventually. I just want to make sure." Very gingerly the kid lowered Pierce until he was sitting. After he straightened, he scampered up the steps and pulled off his sodden robe, laying it out on the chaise to dry, and kicked off his ruined leather sandals.

"Oh geez." Pierce thought of the massacre of perfectly good shoes and robe and was attacked by his conscience, which he'd assumed was dormant or dead. "Kid, I'm sorry about the clothes—"

"Don't be." He shrugged. "They're my old man's, and since he kicked me out of the house for Christmas, he can pretty much kiss off his super classy robe and huaraches, you hear me?"

Pierce wasn't sure whether to chuckle or be horrified. "Just for Christmas?" he asked, making sure.

He lowered the sunglasses over his eyes again, probably to help him look insouciant when he was—in all likelihood—wounded. "Folks were having important political friends over. I'm a gay embarrassment, so I got the beach house. Last year they were in Europe, and I got the beach house with my boyfriend and we fucked like lemmings. No boyfriend this year."

"The lemmings are safe?" Pierce asked, sympathies reluctantly stirred. Parents who judged their kids for sexual activity? He knew those assholes! Pierce and Sasha had grown up with their very own set.

Kid laughed, sounding young and happy instead of casual and cynical. Pierce liked the sound. "Here, let me rub your leg down—I promised."

Pierce grunted. "Kid—"

"Hal—"

"Like the computer?"

Hal stared at him, unimpressed. "Oh dear, a *Space Odyssey* joke. I've never heard one of those, given that I've had this stupid name since birth. Now give me your leg."

Pierce complied, startled by the venom. "Well, I could call you 'Prince Hal,' like—"

"King Henry the Fifth? Like in the Branagh movie?"

Pierce racked his brains, trying to remember. "I thought Branagh just did *Hamlet*," he said, confused.

Hal gasped and wrapped his hands around Pierce's ankle. "Heathen! How could you not know about the Branagh King Henry? He was young and still faithful and downright adorable!"

As he spoke, Hal worked his capable, agile fingers up Pierce's leg—between that and the hot, bubbling water, Pierce's entire body was melting like chocolate in the sun.

"The faithful part is important to you?" Pierce asked, trying to keep his mind on the conversation and not just tilt his head back and drool. Maybe his doctor was missing out on something here. The rubdown in the tub after the physical activity felt like an exciting new way to make a battered body feel whole again.

"Mmhmm… wow." Hal rubbed careful circles around the network of scars on Pierce's knee. "What did you do here?"

"Car accident," Pierce told him again.

"I know that—but here?"

"The door buckled in and ripped up my knee and thigh," Pierce admitted reluctantly. "My arm and shoulder too."

"You were driving," Hal assessed. "What happened?"

Oh, Pierce didn't want to talk about this. "One of those super big trucks ran a red light," he said shortly, and then Hal started rubbing circles at the place where his knee was stiffest. Not the part with the scars, curiously enough—it was like Hal had magic fingers.

"Bummer. Were you alone in the car?"

Ugh. This was what Pierce didn't want to talk about. "My soon-to-be ex-wife," he said, unable to control the loathing.

Hal seemed to hear it anyway—but didn't stop working Pierce's calf and knee. Belatedly, the intimacy of the situation hit Pierce, and he felt stupid. Another human being was touching him, giving him pleasure that was unsolicited by duty or money.

It had been so long.

Pierce closed his eyes and groaned, waiting for Hal to ask the inevitable question.

"Soon-to-be ex?"

It hadn't taken long.

"We were fighting when the truck hit us," Pierce remembered. "When I woke up, Cynthia was hovering over my hospital bed. She said 'Pierce, I forgive you.'"

Hal grunted, eyebrows knitting as he worked on a particularly tough knot.

"That sounds… well, sort of bitchy. What did you say back?"

"I said 'Cynthia, I want a divorce.'"

Hal cackled—and his hands moved up to Pierce's thigh, one hand holding the inner thigh and the other working on the outer.

A charge of heat zinged from Hal's knowing, awesome hands straight to Pierce's groin, and he wondered how embarrassed he'd be if he didn't call a halt to this divine exercise in physical therapy.

Pierce tilted his head back and shuddered and then grabbed Hal's hand—but not hard. "A little personal, a little fast," he said quietly.

Hal grinned, seemingly not put off at all.

"My crowd tends to be a little fast," he said, waggling his eyebrows. Then he winked. "That's okay—taking your time has its advantages too."

Pierce groaned comically and relaxed when Hal went back to his calf. "You don't even know if I'm open for business," he said, trying not to be an asshole. He'd barely gotten out of bed that morning.

"You didn't sock me in the nose. I'm calling it a win!"

Pierce felt sort of a reluctant admiration. "An optimist," he murmured. "Rare species, highly endangered. Usually found in small family groups of quiet suburb dwellers." Pierce remembered Sasha and what an asshole he'd been. Gently he pulled his leg out of Hal's grip.

"What's the matter?" Hal asked as Pierce gathered his noodle-y muscles and rose to pull himself out of the hot tub. "I thought we were getting along so well!"

"We were," Pierce said, hating himself. "But I'm sort of toxic to nice people, and kid, you're just... just really nice. I'm giving you a chance to save yourself some prick burns."

"Huh."

Oh God, the concrete was hard on his feet and joints. He started a slow, determined limp to his chaise, but he couldn't resist. That word was just sitting out there, begging for banter.

"Huh what?"

"No one has ever tried to save me from their inner prick before. Harold Justice Lombard the Fifth is intrigued."

Pierce stopped by a table, catching his balance on the back of one of the chairs. "Is that really your name? And you're an optimist? Holy God, kid, run far away from me—you're like a unicorn or something!"

Before he could even think about moving on, Hal had hopped out of the hot tub and was sprinting for Pierce's stuff. He came trotting back holding Pierce's towel, phone, and oh sweet baby jebus, his padded flip-flops.

"Here." Hal set the flip-flops down so Pierce could step into them and then handed over his cane. While Pierce was getting into his shoes—and finding his balance—Hal wrapped the towel around his shoulders.

"Thank you," Pierce said reluctantly. "That's kind."

Hal came around in front of him and pulled the ends of the towel together, making sure he was wrapped tight.

"Now, I'll see you tomorrow, okay? And don't worry about bringing music, because I'm going to fix you right up. I'll bring Backstreet Boys—that's your generation, right?"

"I'm only thirty-two!" Pierce complained, not sure when he'd agreed to a second workout.

Hal's cheerfully salacious grin told him all he needed to about what he had just inadvertently done. "Excellent. That's truly the best news I've heard all day. I'll bring something good—trust me."

This close, Pierce could see the wickedly sparkling brown eyes behind the sunglasses—and the sudden swallow and slightly parted lips that indicated Hal wasn't quite as bold and brave as he was pretending to be.

It was the vulnerability that did it.

"Sure," Pierce said softly. "I'll be here tomorrow at ten."

And that was enough, apparently, because Hal gave him a toothy grin, then moved to the side and bowed with an elegant gesture. "Then carry on, good sir. We shall see each other in the yon."

Oh geez. What a little hambone.

"Of course, Sir Knight," Pierce returned, resigned to his fate. "Be careful of your unicorn horn, okay? I'd hate to see it broken or bent or anything."

"Will do."

Pierce made better time with the cane and the shoes, and his limp away from the field of battle had a little more dignity this time.

But he was not free from the wonderful world of social interaction—not just yet.

As he approached the back of his condo, he watched an older woman struggle to get her little foldable pull cart full of groceries through the back gate that led to the individual courtyard that was a feature of all the lower-level condos. The gates were tricky—they all had a really strong spring—and Pierce had been forbidden from even trying to wrestle his luggage inside, which was why Sasha and Marshall had done it.

But the elderly woman, dressed flamboyantly in bright magenta and sky blue, didn't have a Sasha and a Marshall, and Pierce figured what the hell—how hard could it be to reach over and hold the gate open, right?

He reached out and pushed, and she hauled her dolly up over the concrete step and into the little patio.

"Thank you," she said shortly.

"Anytime," he told her, waiting patiently for her to clear the gate so he could lower his arm.

"You know, you shouldn't spend too much time with that Lombard kid—he's trouble."

Pierce was surprised enough to let the gate slip out of his fingers, and he scrambled to keep it from crashing into the grumpy old hag and her absurdly stocked shopping cart. Seriously—she had five boxes of protein bars. If she didn't have some laxatives stuffed in that thing, she'd be in a world of hurt.

"I'm sorry?" he asked, trying not to wince as he strained all the muscles he'd just loosened up in the hot tub.

"That Lombard kid. He's—" She looked both ways, like somebody could hear her. "—you know. G-a-y. And he's not quiet about it either! Last year he brought his"—she wrinkled her nose—"boyfriend to the condo, and they were holding hands and snuggling. Perfectly awful, if you ask me."

Ugh. "I didn't, you snotty bitch," Pierce snapped, letting the gate close on her cart.

"Well, I never!"

"You should," Pierce told her, hobbling away. "And while you're at it, buy some laxatives—you'll feel better. Jesus, lady, he's a sweet kid. You really gotta gossip about him like that?"

He had to admit, he got a great deal of satisfaction hearing her swear at her cart and the gate and Pierce all together as he made it through the gate of his own apartment. If he was going to let his inner asshole reach out and touch people, telling that woman off was the way to go.

Besides.

He walked into his condo and leaned back against the door, letting some of the outrage seep from his body.

That sweet kid. Seriously—what had he done to deserve that old biddy and her bitchery? Pierce felt a surge of protectiveness swelling his chest. Yeah, the kid might make more advances, but Pierce was a grown-up. He didn't have to give in. What mattered was Harold Justice Lombard the Fifth didn't have to spend his mornings alone.

Pierce couldn't do much. No job, no wife, no life, right?

But he could be a willing recipient of all that chirpy goodwill.

What could it hurt? Seriously. What could it possibly hurt?

SLIPPERY SLOPES

"I'M DYING!" Pierce complained under the R & B stylings of Jay-Z. For one thing, Jay-Z hadn't been his thing in high school, but for another? He was sure if he did one more underwater leap, his stomach muscles would explode.

"You are not dying!" Hal laughed. "You just can't think of anything better to do!"

"Ugh… if you were older than a minute—"

"I'd still be kicking your ass, old man. Now come on. Your injuries suck, I get it, but we want you to have mobility in a month!"

Pierce stopped dead and almost drowned, then resumed the exercise at a slightly saner pace. "What's a month have to do with it?" he panted, underwater leaping for all he was worth.

"Well, you said you were here until Christmas Eve. I figure you came here to be alone and grumpy and pissed at the world, and you have a month to get over yourself. Mobility will help."

Pierce scowled because that was incredibly astute—but he kept exercising so he might continue to breathe. "Where in the hell did you get that?" he demanded, surly as fuck. He'd shown up that morning all willing to accept Hal's revoltingly happy goodwill and had, instead, been told to suck it up, buttercup, he was going to get his ass beat into the pool.

He'd had no idea such a darling child could be such a sadistic drill sergeant.

"Nine upper division units in psychology. Duh!"

Pierce managed a look at Hal's face and saw the snarky smile that had charmed Pierce in the first place.

"To be a massage therapist?"

"Well, that's just this year," Hal informed him loftily. "I am a man of many ambitions."

"You are a young flake with no direction," Pierce deduced and then felt bad.

Hal shook it off like the proverbial duck. "Well, the massage therapist thing seems to be sticking," he admitted. "I got the certificate online over the summer, and I've been getting my practice hours on the guys on the sports teams at school. And I'm a personal trainer and aqua instructor. I like knowing stuff that'll help me help people."

"Ah, so I'm a project." Well, it made sense. Pierce had never been a looker—long bony jaw, narrow green eyes, sand-brown hair. The accident injuries just made his tall, awkward body look gnarled and misshapen. "It all becomes clear."

He didn't expect Hal to glare at him. "Yeah, well, like anybody over thirty, you can't see for shit. Now tuck and boogie—no, don't bend your knees, keep them straight and kick from the hip!"

Oh ouch. "What in the hell—were you a Roman general in a past life?"

Hal's glare lightened up. "Those guys got play. You realize that, don't you?"

It took Pierce a couple of moves to realize he was talking about sex. "Yeah," he said, remembering something about that in college. "But only the gay or bi ones. No women for them."

Hal crouched down at the pool's edge and took off his sunglasses. "What about you?"

"I may have mentioned an ex-wife?" Pierce was embarrassed about that, actually. The whole divorce was embarrassing. In fact, so was the entire marriage.

"Yeah, but you never said anything about ex-boyfriends," Hal wheedled. "Enquiring minds want to know!"

Oh God. Pierce could just put him off. He *should* just put him off. Or lie. Or not give in to his flirting. But all of Pierce's energy right now was going into keeping up with this goddamned song!

"He was a sweet kid," Pierce muttered. "An optimist. I was too cranky for him. Take a lesson."

But of course that's not what Hal heard. "I knew it!" he crowed, standing up and hopping on the edge of the pool. "I knew you were bent!"

As in "not straight." Of course. "Only a little," Pierce panted. "To the left." He should have hated himself for adding to the play, but

Hal chortled, and he couldn't. So easy to make this kid smile. How long since Pierce thought he was capable of doing that?

A sudden shift in music caught Pierce's attention. "Oh thank God," he muttered to take the conversation away from sex. "Beastie Boys."

"I thought you said you were only thirty-two!" Hal protested, and Pierce would have rolled his eyes, but he might have gotten them wet.

"Beastie Boys are forever!" he proclaimed, and continued to work his ass off to the soul-sweetening strains of "Sabotage."

And then, to make life extra special, Hal gave him Coldplay for the cooldown.

It was like the kid cared.

Of course, Pierce should have known the grilling wouldn't just stop there. He'd hoped, but Hal had proved nothing if not relentless.

"So," he said slyly while working Pierce's leg over in the hot tub. "Bent?"

Pierce grunted. "College-try bi," he said flippantly, and Hal rewarded him with a thumb right in the middle of his arch. "Augh! Okay! Okay!" Hal fixed the cramp with his palm, and after a few moments, Pierce took a deep breath and closed his eyes. "Loren. Loren Simpson. We met in our senior year, and we were both between girlfriends, and…." And… he could picture Loren's face—blue eyes, earnestness, the fever flush that came over him when he came. "He was sweet," Pierce said simply. "For a little while, it was true love."

"Why'd it end?" Hal asked, his hands almost too gentle on Pierce's calf to do any good.

"He was premed. I was engineering." Pierce still remembered that day—the day they'd realized it wouldn't work out. The ache in his chest that hadn't quit for a month, the way Loren had kept wiping his eyes with the back of his hand.

The transported, almost ethereal expression on Loren's face as he came inside Pierce for the last time.

"So you broke up?" Hal sounded indignant, and Pierce opened his eyes and regarded his young friend with a sadness he couldn't shake.

"It was the grown-up decision," he said, and it sounded like a cop-out now, when it hadn't back in school. "I had a job offer already from Hewlett-Packard, Loren had been accepted to Stanford. His parents would have cut off his support if he'd come out—"

"What about yours?" Hal asked perceptively.

Pierce wanted to shrug, but he couldn't. "Oh, mine would have—most definitely. But I didn't really care about mine. They were assholes. I cut off contact with them about a year later anyway. But Loren… it meant a lot to him. All of it. Med school, Stanford, Mom and Dad. I couldn't… you know."

Hal shook his head, looking angry. "You didn't fight for him?" he asked, sounding forlorn.

"Oh, kid. Is that what happened to you?"

Hal turned away, his hands completely still.

"We made a decision together. He didn't want me to fight for him. He told me himself." Pierce remembered how hard he'd fought that. The part of him that died when he resigned himself to the breakup. "But I wasn't happy about it," he admitted.

Hal had perched his sunglasses on the top of his head when they'd gotten into the hot tub, and now he lowered them again before turning back to look at Pierce. No doubt his eyes were red rimmed.

"So, you would have fought for him," Hal said, like this mattered to him a great deal.

It was on the tip of his tongue to say "No, eventually we all give up." He hated to disillusion the kid. But he couldn't forget Sasha, showing up at his apartment a year after school, saying she was pregnant. Pierce had fought for her, hadn't he? Yeah, he'd apparently become a real festering cold sore since, but once, just once in his life, he'd fought for someone, and he'd made a difference.

"Yeah," he said, because here, under the gray haze of late November in Florida, he could remember wanting to fight. The need to be with someone he truly cared about had boiled in his blood then, no matter how thin that blood was now.

"Good," Hal said, nodding. Then he went back to Pierce's feet, but by now the nerves were too raw. Pierce pulled away.

"Sorry—my feet are about done."

"The tile floors, right?" Hal nodded like it was a foregone conclusion. "They're great because you can sweep all the sand out when you walk on the beach, but they're hell on your body."

Pierce grunted. Just getting out of bed hurt.

"Tell you what." Hal grinned perkily. "Tomorrow we'll do a light workout, mostly stretching, then we can go buy mats."

Duh. "Like rubber mats?" Hey, that had been his idea too!

"Oh yeah—the kind they have at the gym should do. You can cut them to size—they'll make walking on those floors so much easier, trust me." His melancholia over Pierce's apparent failure to believe in true love had melted, and damn. The kid was offering to do him a solid.

"Sure," Pierce said, because otherwise tomorrow was doing a whole lot of what he'd done over the last two days. "Maybe I can get a chair too." Derrick had a small work desk in the living room, but he apparently used a kitchen chair to work there. Pierce had taken one look at that setup and known it would break his fragile, healing body. "I can start... I don't know. Looking up jobs or something."

"Here in Florida?" Hal asked, sounding eager.

"Naw." Pierce shrugged. "I've got a house in Sacramento. It's small, but I got to keep it and most of the furniture after the divorce." He smiled a little, remembering the den that he got to outfit all on his own. "The bedroom is fucking pink, but the den is nice. All hardwood and paneling. A work desk and a big gaming TV." His smile faded. It was the first time he'd thought happily of home since he'd awakened in the hospital. Sasha had come out when he'd called her, after Cynthia had stormed out of his room, and she'd met him at discharge with enough pain pills to get him on the plane, along with all the luggage she could pack.

God bless his sister. He'd paid her back so poorly.

"Oh." Hal's shoulders sagged. Then he perked up. "I've never been to California. Maybe I could visit."

That suddenly, Pierce needed to know about Hal for a change. "Where do your parents live?" he asked, thinking the kid seemed to need to get away a lot.

"North Carolina," Hal muttered, like the state name was a dirty word. Well, when you were young and gay, maybe it was right now. "My father's a judge."

Yikes.

"A conservative judge?" Pierce asked, just to make sure.

"Is there any other kind?"

"I had a liberal judge let me off a traffic ticket once," Pierce told him, just to ease some of the bitterness.

Hal grinned at him. "In California?"

"Yeah. In California." Pierce winked and then sighed. "Well, the heat has effectively sucked all the energy from my bones, and it's time for me to go take my nap."

"Oh God—I'm sorry. Here—let me help you out."

Pierce didn't refuse his help per se, just tried to do most of the work himself. He leaned heavily on the rail and took solid, shuffling steps on his own, trying to get to the table. Finally Hal huffed in exasperation.

"I'm stronger than I look, okay? Just lean on me a little. Jesus, what could happen?"

"I could put too much weight on you, you could overbalance, I could land wrong and call you a horrible name that I'll regret for the rest of my life," Pierce snarled. "You seem to like me a little—at the moment, it's the only win I've got."

Oh dammit dammit dammit—way to go and injure the frickin' unicorn, Pierce!

But his unicorn wasn't looking cowed or wounded or any of the things Sasha had.

"Well, it's not much of a win if you don't trust me to hold some of your weight. Now come on—here!" Hal tucked his hand under Pierce's elbow, and Pierce had no choice. He leaned. Together they made it to the table, where his cane sat accusingly, as did the sandals that would protect his feet from the deck.

Hal helped him balance as he slid his feet into the flip-flops. "I really did put you through your paces," he said grudgingly. "You did it all like a champ, but you should carb up a little when you get back to your condo. What're you going to have for lunch?"

Pierce thought about the groceries Sasha and Marshall had brought over. "Can of soup and some crackers," he announced, because hey—he had enough of that stuff to last him for four more days if he ate it day and night, like he had been.

"Not good enough," Hal said grimly, handing him his cane and then wrapping his towel over his shoulders. "Lead me to your condo, oh emaciated one—let me see your stores."

Oh... hell no. No. "I know you have something better to do," Pierce told him, hating feeling this vulnerable.

Hal appeared to think about it. "Hm... meeting world leaders for lunch, solving hunger for dinner, penning my novel before I go to bed... but right the hell now, I really only have to go see if my neighbor has anything to eat before he starves himself to death because he's a stubborn asshole!"

"I have food," Pierce muttered. "You don't need to worry about me."

"Oh, but I do." Hal took off his sunglasses with his free hand and batted his eyelashes. They stood close enough that Pierce could see the true, remarkable gold-brown of his eyes.

His throat went dry. "I'd rather not be an object of pity," he said, knowing he couldn't be more pathetic if he tried.

"Then let me feed you so I don't feel sorry for you," Hal said sweetly, but he was standing very still and staring at Pierce soberly.

Pierce nodded just to break the moment—them, frozen, staring at each other. But nothing could erase the heat of Hal's skin as he continued to escort Pierce down the sidewalk.

"Nobody uses the pool," Pierce mumbled, realizing this was their second day alone.

"Later," Hal told him, surprisingly. "A few people come out to sun themselves later. But it's not prime condo season right now."

Pierce grunted and continued his trek. "The holidays."

"Yeah."

The word had the ring of loneliness in it, and Pierce looked at him in question. But this time it was Hal's turn to be looking away.

"You, uh... spending the holidays here—that wasn't your idea, was it?"

He shrugged. "Told you—too gay to be an asset."

"Is that, uh, just for the holidays, or is that for the rest of the year?"

Hal grimaced. "Let's just say that next semester, I am enrolled in fifteen credits of poli sci at UNC and leave it at that."

It was like watching the pictures on a slot machine whir and click… wanted to be a masseur or a fitness trainer—cherry. Too gay for the holidays—cherry. Twenty-three and not done with school—cherry and jackpot!

"If you don't do what they want you to do, they'll cut you off," Pierce muttered. "Charming."

"Whatever. I told them I'd come here and think about it."

Pierce remembered Hal's outfit on the first day and felt a chill in his stomach. "Don't you mean drink about it?" he asked kindly.

"Yeah, well, that. Except…." Hal kicked at a piece of gravel as they neared the gate of the condo.

"What?" Because now Pierce was curious.

"I hate getting drunk. Seriously. I like training and helping people and shit. You can't do that if you're going to destroy your body. So I bought, like, all this fucking vodka, and after the first three greyhounds, I trashed the place. I fell asleep. I woke up and decided to take a swim and… well, you were already here."

"Trashed the place? Do you need to clean up?"

"When I'm not so mad, I'll do it again, sure. But I'm not drinking any more vodka after that."

Pierce stepped forward to undo the lock on the gate and laughed. "Well, lucky for us both. You don't like to get drunk, and I'm not happy about drowning. It was kismet."

Hal pushed through the gate and held it while Pierce limped by. "You don't agree with my dad? That I should get my ass in gear and pick something?"

Pierce thought about it as he led the way through the back hallway, past the laundry room, the bedroom, and into the kitchen that opened up to the living room. He paused there—he always did—because the back door looked over a brace of rushes and off to the sea. While the sea in Florida was a little tamer than the sea in California, that didn't mean he couldn't appreciate having it right there at his window. Of course, he hadn't this trip—because pain and bitterness and general assholery, but that didn't mean he couldn't start *now*.

"No," he said, almost absently, pondering that view. He snapped to and answered with more conviction. "I think that whole 'your kid has to do what you tell them, even as an adult' idea is sort of... bullshit," he said. "I mean, you support them, sure. Hold them accountable. But you're obviously not partying the fuck out of UNC. How many units do you have?"

Hal grunted. "Well, if I had them in the right classes, I'd have a master's by now."

Pierce laughed and settled down onto one of the stools that sat at the counter. "I... I always wanted more time to think about it," he said, remembering. "I mean, I took a film theory class and some history classes and thought 'Hey! I'd like to do something with this!' But I was tired of eating soup and crackers five nights a week and driving a car that was writing its last will and testament. I mean, if I could have gone to school for another three years, I totally would have."

Hal's smile still had an edge of unhappiness to it, but Pierce didn't know what to tell him. "Here—let me see what's for lunch," he said. He began poking around the pantry and the cupboards, clucking when he came up with english muffins and lunch meat. "You were going to have tinned soup? Here, let me make you a sandwich. You even have a tomato and pickles. And butter! Geez."

Pierce stood up and tried not to groan theatrically. "Hal.... Hal... bubby... the reason I was going for canned soup was that I didn't feel like making anything. I can't ask you to—"

"I'll make myself one too," Hal said mildly. "Now sit there and talk to me about something stupid."

"Something stupid?"

"Yeah." Hal looked up from his food preparation, and Pierce realized he wasn't kidding, even a little. "Something that doesn't hurt."

Oh. Well, at least Pierce wasn't the only one not comfortable with all the soul baring they'd done in the last two days.

Pierce bit his lip, trying to remember something, anything, whimsical that he could talk about. All he had in his arsenal was stuff from when he was a kid.

"So," he said, feeling foolish, "have I talked to you about my deep and abiding love for the old Looney Tunes cartoons?"

Hal shot him a look of such naked hope, he felt like an absolute hero for even thinking about it. "Bugs Bunny or Daffy Duck?" he asked.

"Wabbit season, naturally."

Hal's smile turned wicked. "Duck season," he returned.

"Wabbit season."

"Duck season."

"Duck season!" Pierce remembered this game.

"Bang," Hal told him with a smile. Derrick had a widescreen TV on the far wall, and Hal gestured with his chin. "I bet you could find some of that on a premium channel. Go, sit—I'll bring you food, you eat and fall asleep."

"I'm not—" Pierce yawned. "Dammit!"

"Yeah, well, I really did work you hard." Hal bit his lip in an expression that was starting to look more and more vulnerable. "Thanks for letting me. Like I said, tomorrow we'll do something lighter, and we can go shopping."

"That's sounds...." Oh wait. Shopping. And it was getting close to Christmas! "Hey—can we get more than rubber mats and a chair?"

Hal crossed his expressive brown eyes. "No, then I'll have to dump your ass at the store. Why, what did you have in mind?"

"Well, you know. Christmas is coming. I'd like to sort of spoil my sister's family a little. She's got kids. They're not bad. Maybe get her an espresso machine or something. She and her husband power up with Mr. Coffee—it's horrible."

"So, rubber mats, Legos, Barbies, and a Keurig? It's a good thing I've got a CR-V—if I'd gone for the Tesla I'd wanted, you'd be fucked."

Pierce blushed, feeling exploitive. "I'm sorry—you know, we don't have to do that. I can order their stuff from here—it'll even show up gift-wrapped—"

"No," Hal said, like he was surprised the idea pleased him too. "Don't do that. I mean, even if we don't get to everything tomorrow, it will... it will give us a quest." His full and beaming smile emerged, the one that made Pierce think he was an invincible unicorn. "Even if we are thwarted in our first sally, Sir Knight, we shall continue to assail

the indomitable fortress of consumerism until we have achieved...
uh, gift-tasticness?"

Pierce shrugged. "Or redemption. You know, either-or?"

"Redemption?" Pierce could practically see Hal's antennae rise
up. "For what?"

Pierce stood and managed the trek across the tile to the coffee
table. He didn't want to talk about it—not today, when they'd
discovered some neutral ground.

"I thought we were watching cartoons," he said gently.

"Yeah." Hal swallowed, and his smile dimmed. "You're right.
Cartoons—we need to figure out which season it is."

Pierce made himself comfortable and welcomed the sandwich
and glass of milk when Hal walked it over. They watched cartoons for
the next hour, laughing like children at the basic slapstick humor. As
Pierce dozed off, slumping sideways onto the pillows of the couch, he
couldn't remember the last time he'd felt that young.

He woke up to late-afternoon shadows, cuddled under a throw in
a chilly, empty apartment. The sound of the sea washed hypnotically
through his bones like it did every minute of every day here. A note
sat on the marble coffee table in front of him.

*Thanks for the company—I'll give you a Hal break tonight, but
see you bright and early tomorrow.*

—H

Pierce sat up, feeling unexpectedly refreshed, and pondered
the note.

A Hal break? Who said he needed a break from Hal? He was
starting to sort of like Hal. Why would he want a break?

He shivered and stood up, dislodging the chenille throw as he
went to turn on the lights in the living room. He stared at the thing,
trying to place where it had come from, and then he realized—

Derrick kept his spare blankets in the linen closet between the
bathroom and the bedroom. Hal had needed to go looking for that.
He'd done it on purpose, to make sure Pierce was comfortable, after
he'd made Pierce a meal and entertained him.

Pierce couldn't stop looking at the throw as it lay crumpled on
the floor.

What season was it?

It was denial season.

HE GOT up eventually and made himself a can of soup and then settled back down in front of the television, remote in hand. His phone buzzed, the sound so alien of late that he barely recognized it before he remembered to pick up.

"Derrick?"

"Are you dead?"

"Oh God. No." Pierce sat up from his sprawl and stretched carefully. "I'm sorry—I got here two days ago. I should have called."

"Yeah, well, I was in a turkey coma until yesterday, so you're doing okay. How are you?"

Pierce grunted. "Better," he confessed. Derrick knew why he'd come here—had been the one to calm him down after Pierce had blown up at Sasha. Derrick had told him then that it wasn't unforgivable, but Pierce—he still felt the shame down in his gut.

"As in no longer suicidal?" Derrick asked sharply.

Pierce flushed. "I wasn't that bad," he mumbled. "It was just… I was an asshole. I didn't want to expose her to me being an asshole to her in her own house. Wasn't her fault. How's Miranda?"

Derrick's wife, bless her, should have divorced Pierce's best friend a long time ago, because she was way too damned good for him. "She's fine. Or she will be when she recovers from the humiliation. Apparently she forgot to put enough sugar in one of the damned pies. Her family won't let her live it down. If one more jackass calls me with an offer to bring over a cup of sugar, I'm gonna go fuckin' ballistic."

Pierce grimaced. "Ouch. Family."

"What a fuckin' bag of dicks."

Pierce had to laugh. "Yeah, well, witness."

"Shut up. You and Sasha give me hope. None of these assholes would have let a thing like that slow them down."

Well, there was a reason Derrick was his best friend. That and— "How's work?" Pierce asked before he could stop himself.

Derrick cackled. "Missing the hell out of you, that's for sure. Speaking of assholes…." Well, layoffs had been coming, and Pierce had the bad luck to crash his truck about a week before they arrived. He'd been pretty sure he hadn't been on the list before he'd been taken out of commission, but who could prove what?

Pierce gusted out a breath. "Yeah, well, sadly it's mutual." He'd liked his job designing graphics chips for video game players—he and his team, Derrick included, had worked really well together.

"Well, I know you're doing okay for money," Derrick said frankly, because he'd gotten a year's worth of severance at the layoff—and both Pierce and the guy who'd hit him had good insurance that had paid out. "But I also know you, and that's the whole reason I called."

"Besides making sure I wasn't dead," Pierce said dryly.

"Well, that too. Anyway—there's a smaller company out here putting out feelers. Young, hot, fresh—willing to blow you if you promise to come, that sort of thing. Anyway, I gave them your card. They're going to be emailing you in a couple of days. Try not to fuck this up."

Pierce gasped, suddenly almost tearful. "A job? You got me a job?"

"No, I dropped your name. Don't be dramatic. And I told them you wouldn't be back until March of next year too, so don't blow the first vacation you've had in years."

Pierce gave a rusty laugh. "I'm still rehabilitating," he reminded his friend. "No promises I'll be 100 percent ever, you know that."

"Can you walk?" Derrick demanded. "Can you use a computer?"

"Yes and yes," Pierce told him promptly, thinking about the range of motion he could feel in his legs after two days of decent aqua therapy.

"Then the rest is improvement. Anyway—you'll have time."

"I will." Pierce felt his throat get thick again. "Thank you. Just, seriously, thank you. That's… that's awesome."

"Just tell me you aren't rotting at my beach condo eating canned soup and trying to die alone."

"No." Pierce felt the corners of his mouth turn up without meaning to make that happen. "In fact, I think I made a friend."

"Hm… promising." Derrick was sort of a midsize man with a thatch of blond hair and a goatee, and Pierce could picture him stroking his goatee. "Would this be a friend with tits that you can sleep with?"

Pierce grunted. "Doesn't need breasts—you know that."

Derrick grunted back. "I forget. I'm a straight white male who tries not to have entitlement issues—pity me."

Oh God. Derrick and Miranda probably gave 10 percent of their income to liberal causes. "I refuse to pity you now that I've been repressed," Pierce told him grandly. "But seriously, a friend. That's all I could ask for, and I'm calling it a win."

"But is it a cute friend? That's all I'm asking," Derrick needled, and Pierce gave in.

"He's really sort of adorable."

Derrick's cackle was all he ever wanted in a buddy. "Excellent! I see good things in your future, my man. I shall leave you alone so I can go impregnate my wife!"

Pierce blinked. "Was that, uh, something you'd planned on doing?"

And suddenly the joking fell away. "We're hoping," his friend confessed. "Are you happy for us?"

"Only if I'm invited to the birth." Pierce waited a moment to see if he'd gone too far, but Derrick's howl of mock outrage reassured him.

"Oh, you dickhead! I love you so! Yes, I'll tell Miranda right now that's a priority!"

Pierce's laugh surprised him—two days ago he would have said it was beyond him.

What a difference a Hal made.

"Don't tell her that or you'll never conceive. Now go! Be nice to your wife." His voice dropped. "And good luck, man. You guys… you're the best."

"So are you. Come back to us, 'kay? If I take Miranda to one more Kings' game, she'll divorce me."

"Understood."

Derrick hung up, and Pierce was left in the empty condo again. But his laughter still rang on the cold tile, and Pierce could hear Hal's reaction to the conversation he'd just had.

Hey, Hal—I have friends! We're actually funny together!

He suddenly wanted his young friend to see him when he wasn't angry and bitter.

He wanted Hal to know he could be fun too, and not just when Looney Tunes was on.

PUBLIC WORKS

"HEY, HAL—WHO'S that?"

Hal looked up from the rack of jeans he was perusing—in Pierce's size—and glanced in the same direction Pierce was. "I have no idea."

The kid—um, young man—Hal's age sported a brownish man bun and a scarf around his white T-shirted neck and had been cruising Hal with raised eyebrows and a predatory gleam since they'd arrived at the outlet mall. Now as Hal looked over his shoulder, the guy winked and smiled coquettishly.

Hal rolled his eyes and turned back to Pierce. "Now see, if we weren't in Tommy Hilfiger, he wouldn't have seen us, and I wouldn't have to scrape him like a barnacle. So you need to just concede to the inevitable and let me buy you pants that don't look like dad jeans."

Pierce let out a little whine. "I thought we'd be at Target or something—at least for the rubber mats and the office chair."

Hal looked at him unhappily. "Crap. Would you believe I forgot that's why we came? I was just so damned excited to go somewhere with you."

Oh no. Pierce grimaced. "Look, I don't want to piss on your parade, but—"

"But you don't want to waste time doing something not practical. I get it." Hal snapped his sunglasses on over his eyes and turned toward the exit, self-recrimination etched in every line of his body.

"No!" Pierce laughed, wondering where that wound had come from. "Not at all. I'm actually having a really good time, even if you apparently think I look like hell."

"Really?" Hal turned back and slid the sunglasses up to the top of his head again. "Then what is it?"

Pierce shrugged, embarrassed. Hal had kept his promise about giving him a light stretching workout that morning—Pierce had felt invigorated as he'd clumped to the condo, showered, and put on a pair of jeans and a Hawaiian shirt—by far the dressiest things he owned. Hal's good-natured ribbing about the dad jeans had prompted Pierce to offer to buy some more clothes—and then Hal had offered to buy them for him.

They'd had fun until just this minute. "I... I've got maybe two stores in me," he said apologetically. "If one of them is here and the other one is Target, I'm going to have to get a Lyft into town to go Christmas shopping." *Ugh.* "Sorry—I'm just trying to get as much as possible out of my freeloading here."

Hal smacked his forehead. "Doh! Okay—good. I mean, not good that I totally forgot your agenda like a punk, but good that you made that clear. Gotcha. Tell you what. Let's get you some clothes—because... dude."

"Understood," Pierce said dryly. Cynthia hadn't liked the way he'd dressed either—but then, she hadn't made him laugh when they'd gone shopping. If she'd tried to make it fun, even a little, talking about movie stars with consummate bitchery or joking about how a yellow shirt would make him look like Tweety Bird, Pierce might have stepped up his game.

"Then we'll go out to lunch—they've got the best café here. I'm dying to take you. Afterward we'll go to Target. I know where the rubber matting is—I bought a shit-ton for my place a couple of years ago, and you can find the office chair of your dreams. Then, you work out heavy for the next two days, and we try this again after that?"

Pierce smiled, flattered. "You wouldn't mind taking me back? I'm, uh"—he gestured to the whole store—"I'm sort of a clod, you know."

Hal winked. "Yeah, but you're willing to be trained up. That's my favorite sort of clod. And seriously, I'm having fun. Just let me know if your leg or your hip gets too stiff. I'll go look for stuff and bring it to you in the dressing room, okay?"

"That's... that's really nice." Suddenly Pierce wanted to cry. "You're really good at this planning stuff, you know? Babying my weak ass? It's... it's nice, that's all."

Oh! He'd never seen such preening. But since Hal was preening as he held up decent-looking shirts in his size, Pierce was going to call it a win.

He tried on two pairs of jeans and three shirts, awkwardly taking things on and off in the cramped dressing room while his semiabused body ached. He held out the one pair of jeans that fit and said, "I'll get these, okay?"

"What about the shirts?" Hal asked, taking the jeans and scrupulously not looking at Pierce's bare and scarred body in the cubicle.

"Well, the blue one fits and looks pretty good, the red one is too tight, and the yellow one…. Tweety Bird and me should not be friends."

"Gotcha. I'll go get these—"

"No, no." Pierce waved him off. "No—this was a good idea, and it was fun, and I'm the one getting the clothes. I'll get them."

Hal *hmm*ed noncommittally. "Just get dressed," he said mildly. "I'll meet you at checkout."

Pierce met him at the cash stand, where Hal presented him with the bag of already purchased items—plus another pair of jeans and three shirts in the same size.

And a belt.

"Aw, man!" Pierce said, looking through the bag's contents. "That's not—"

"It was my choice," Hal said, only the faintest bit of rebellion in his tone. "Here—let me carry the bag. We can go eat at the spicy seafood place, and you can promise that next time we go out, you'll look less like a suburban dad and more like a hot guy in his thirties."

Pierce wrapped both mental hands around his misanthropy and asked patiently, "Why? Why is it so important to you that I don't look like a suburban dad?"

Hal scowled—and the look was surprisingly effective on him. "'Cause that guy scoping me out was shady, that's why. For all he knows, we're on a date, and I don't like anyone throwing shade on you."

"You did see him!" He knew it!

"Well, yeah. But it's rude. People used to do that to Russ and me all the time."

"Try to poach you from your boyfriend?" Pierce was lost.

"No. Try to poach Russ. He's sort of a model, and he's really frickin' beautiful. And he used to laugh it off, like it was no big deal. And then…." He shook his head. "Here. The spicy fried fish is to die for. I'd do that."

Pierce was just grateful to hobble through the outdoor mall into the bar-style restaurant and sit down. Lord, it was sixty degrees outside, but the humidity and the glare of the sun made it feel about eighty. He really hated the trickle of sweat that crept from his neck to between his shoulder blades to disappear under the waistband of his jeans and haunt the crack of his ass.

A perky waitress with thick blonde hair in twin french braids seated them and took their drink orders, leaving Pierce to look around, grateful they'd arrived in the afternoon lull.

"Mm…," he said, closing his eyes and turning his face toward the fan. "Air conditioning."

Hal laughed, some of his earlier bitterness fading away. "You Californians—you're easy to please," he said, and Pierce waggled his eyebrows.

"Yup. You have no idea."

"Maybe someday." Hal winked and looked at the menu. "So, the spicy fried fish—"

"They've got a fish and chips plate with it?"

"Yup—right there. It's big enough for two if you want to split it."

Oh perfect. "You read my mind."

They set their menus down, and Pierce wondered whether or not to break their little bubble by asking the hard question.

Then Hal said, "Yes, he cheated on me. A lot. And the thing is, I believed him when he said it wasn't personal. He just got… lured. I mean, it was his fault, but he was like a dog chasing a cat and running into the street. Just never saw the bad thing coming, not even when it was fucking him, you know?"

Ouch. "I'm sorry." Pierce meant it with all his heart.

Hal shrugged and fiddled with his water glass. "You didn't do it. You wouldn't do it, either, would you." The surety in his voice was flattering, and for once Pierce didn't have to worry about disillusioning him.

"Nope. Cynthia and I did not have that problem." Odd how it had never occurred to him, not even when things were really bad.

"Then what was the problem?" Hal asked.

The waitress arrived with their iced teas—Hal's sweetened, Pierce's unsweetened with lemonade added—and they gave their orders. Hal added an order of fried calamari because he said it was really wonderful and not on the platter, and then she left and they were alone.

With that question hanging between them.

For a breath, a heartbeat, Pierce thought about refuting the question. Claiming it was too personal. Asking to talk about something stupid.

All he had to do was say "Wabbit season," and this convo never had to happen.

But Hal had bought him clothes. Not because he didn't think Pierce was presentable, really, but to defend his honor.

What an absurdly sweet thing to do.

Pierce would have rather paid for the clothes—especially since Derrick's contact had gotten back to him that morning and practically slobbered all over the cyberwaves at his expertise. He had a settlement from the insurance company, a settlement from the old job—and a new job in the works.

He could have bought his own goddamned clothes.

But Hal apparently had money of his own. What he wanted—what he really wanted—seemed to be friendship.

And that came with telling embarrassing stories about where you decided to draw the line.

"She was judgy as fuck," Pierce said boldly.

"So that's a deal breaker?" Hal asked, cringing. No doubt he was thinking about his earlier celebrity bitchery, but that wasn't what Pierce was talking about.

"You know how you said your ex didn't mean it personally? About cheating?"

Hal nodded, looking troubled. "Yeah. I mean, he meant it every time he said it was the last. I sort of felt bad for him in the end, but I couldn't do it anymore."

"See—she would never have forgiven like that. I mean, you broke up with him, and good for you—but she wouldn't have been okay with it inside. She would have told her mom and her sister and her entire extended family, talking about the cheating again and again and again, and how awful it was and what a horrible human being the cheater was, and then she would have pulled out a bible verse or quoted some prominent writer or politician and… and never, not once, would there have been an acknowledgment, I guess, that the guy was human. Not once."

"But you didn't cheat," Hal said, confused. "So why is this a deal?"

"Because it wasn't just cheating!" Pierce burst out. "It was…." *Oh hell.* "See, my sister, who is the sweetest woman in the world and lives with her equally sweet husband and two adorable kids—she got pregnant at eighteen. And it wasn't easy. I mean, Sasha and I both stopped talking to our parents about it because, dude! They were horrible to her. And I'd just gotten my job at Hewlett-Packard, and I supported her while Marshall worked on getting them an apartment, and we tried to get them cars that worked. She could have gone home, I guess, but they were just hell-bent on making her 'pay.' Like having to deal with a kid while you're getting through college isn't payment enough?"

"Yeah, that'd be rough," Hal said, nodding. "And she had another one?"

Pierce shrugged. "You know, they were married by then and had jobs, but even if they didn't—whose business is it to say it's a bad thing? It's like you and your parents. Why should they get to tell you that you're too gay for Christmas? I think that's horrible. And Cynthia—she just didn't let it go. So I'm talking to Sasha over the computer, and I say something about a business trip I might have to take to Korea, and Sasha… she's never been out of the country, right? She gets really wistful, like, 'Oh yeah, I'd love to do that,' and Cynthia—who is just walking around behind me, putting away laundry—goes, 'Well, you shouldn't have gotten knocked up!'"

"Oh ouch!" Hal stared at him with wide horrified eyes. "What. A. Twat."

"Right?" Oh, Pierce had been wrong. This wasn't something that needed to be hidden. This was something he needed to get off his chest! "And I managed to get off the call with Sasha, but Cynthia and I—well, we fought for the next two days. We fought over dinner, and we fought while we showered. And all I was saying was, judging people is a really shitty way to go through life. And all she kept repeating was that if people didn't want to be judged, they shouldn't fuck up."

Hal cringed again, and Pierce felt a surge of affection for him that had not a thing to do with his warm brown eyes and lush pink mouth or the new clothes leaning against Pierce's calf as he sat. "I'm not wrong, am I?"

"Not from my view," Hal said sincerely. "But—and I'm not being judgy—"

Pierce smiled, appreciating him.

"—but this didn't occur to you before you got married?"

Pierce blew out a breath. "She was my first relationship after Loren," he said simply. "And I was so damned lonely. And she… she could be really kind. I just never saw the strings attached until it was too late."

"Was that the only reason?" Hal asked after a pause. "Because divorcing someone for just one flaw, that seems sort of…."

"Judgy?" Pierce finished, then grew thoughtful. "There was more. There was… I guess there was just this sort of… I want to say superficiality, but that's not the word. Like I said—she could be kind. Her best friend in the world was a big girl—plain and shy—but whenever she came over, I watched Cynthia just light up, and I could tell that when she looked at Wendy, she was seeing an angel from heaven, you know? So she had depth, and she was capable of really nice moments. But it was like she needed a list—she needed someone to tell her what was right and what was wrong, and if she had permission to think it was wrong, boy, did she do that shit up right, you know?"

Hal nodded, looking thoughtful. "I do." He flashed a smile. "Father's a judge, right?"

"Yeah. It was that kind of thing too. The law was the law was the law—but there was no... no understanding that the law could be changed. It's like...."

Pierce searched hard for a simile—it was just such a hard idea to pinpoint.

"Like, when I was in high school, my best friend, Derrick—the guy whose condo I'm currently freeloading in—his older sister got pregnant right when her husband was deployed."

Hal grimaced. "Is it just me, or do you know a lot of pregnant women?"

"That kid just turned sixteen, give me a break. Anyway—Derrick's sister called the school and begged him to take her to the doctor when she went into labor, but he didn't have a car, and I did. So we left school—just left. I didn't call my folks, he didn't call his, 'cause we were kids and hey, lady with a baby."

"Well, yeah." Hal took a pull of his iced tea. "They scare me too."

"They're not so bad—seriously. Derrick and his wife want to have kids. I'm rooting for them. I'll get to play with kids that I don't have to take home with me. It'll be brilliant."

"But about leaving school at seventeen?" Hal was good at keeping up with him.

"We got her to the hospital, and we were even in the room with her until their parents got there. And the next day we go back to school, feeling like heroes, and—"

"You got detention for ditching out on school."

Pierce stared at him. "For two weeks. How did you guess?"

"Because. It was a story about rules and why some of them are stupid. And I got it. I mean... I get it. It's a good analogy." Hal was gazing at him now with a sort of softness in his eyes.

Pierce's face heated. "Sorry. Just... haven't been out with a friend in a while. I... I was talking too much."

"No," Hal said. "You... it's just, I saw the end coming, and I felt bad. You were a unicorn once too."

And that flush wouldn't quit. "I had my moments," he mumbled. Oh God, he really had talked too much.

Hal's smile went quietly blinding. "You'll have more."

Pierce's throat went dry, and he was sucking the dregs of his Arnold Palmer when the waitress came by with the food and two plates.

The mood, successfully broken, lightened up with discussions of amazing spices in the breading and other great things to eat. By the time they were done, Hal had Pierce nodding his head and saying yes to chicken and waffles when they went out again in three days, and that sudden bolt of intimacy between them was forgotten.

Or over.

Maybe not forgotten.

THE TRIP to Target didn't take long, and they emerged victorious with a box of the rubberized mesh mats and an office chair. By the time they got to the car, though, Pierce was limping fiercely, and the arm holding the cane was cramping too.

"Oh man," Hal muttered as he piloted his CR-V over the skyway to the outer beach. "I'm so sorry. All you asked was for stuff to make your condo not awful. I didn't mean to break you."

Pierce let out a weak laugh. "Don't apologize," he said, meaning it. "It was my best day in a long time."

Hal darted a look at him before looking back at traffic. "You mean that?"

"Yeah. Why wouldn't I?"

Hal just shook his head. "Tell you what. We get back, you sit and watch television while I put the mats all over the place. Then I can make us some dinner while we watch TV."

It was such an easy plan—simple and domestic. Hal made him put on sleep pants and a T-shirt and watch the TV in the bedroom with a prop behind his back while he ran around and put the mats down. Dinner was an english muffin sandwich again, and Pierce started dozing off not long after, but he pulled himself awake long enough to say, "You don't have to leave. Watch as much TV as you want."

"I need to look some stuff up on my computer," Hal said. "If you give me the keys, I can go get it and come back."

"Sure. They're on the counter." Sometime after that, in his dreams, he felt the brief touch of fingertips on his temple as he slept, but he was too tired to open his eyes and see if it was real.

He woke up in the middle of the night to use the bathroom and realized Hal had taken him at his word. The bed—a giant king-sized pedestal affair that made Pierce think of sleeping on the divan of the gods—was big enough that Pierce hadn't even realized that sometime in the night, Hal had just stretched out in a pair of sweats, covering up with the throw he'd pulled out a few days before. He was huddled under it now, like he was cold.

After Pierce hobbled to the bathroom, he took a mild painkiller—the cramping in his leg and arm hadn't eased up, and he had to concede he'd overdone it. The good news was, the rubber matting under his feet softened the impact against the tile, and what used to feel like a death march without his flip-flops was now just averagely uncomfortable. After the painkiller, he went to the linen cupboard and grabbed one more afghan.

He paused on the way back to bed. He hadn't drawn the blinds in front of the sliding glass door to the beach, and for a moment he stood, mesmerized by the view of the moonlight, bright against the black sky and luminous on the water.

"Whatcha doin'?" Hal mumbled from the room behind him.

Pierce turned and smiled, because he sounded sleepy and dear. "Nothing. Taking an Advil. Get under the covers, baby—you're cold."

"Mm'kay."

Pierce walked back into the room and laid the throw at the foot of the bed in case they got cold, then crawled in. He turned toward Hal, wondering if he'd feel anything about having a man in his bed again, but Hal was on the edge, not even close enough for Pierce to feel his body heat.

He closed his eyes, letting the painkiller do its work.

In that honest moment between sleeping and dreaming, he was brave enough to admit that it would be nice to roll over and snuggle that hard young body, to bury his nose in the hollow of

Hal's shoulder and see what he smelled like when he was warm and soft in the dark.

HAL TOOK Pierce's rehabilitation damned seriously.

He'd upped the workout—Pierce was at an hour and a half now, much of it stretching, with more stretching in the hot tub.

Hal always got in and rubbed him down, hands solicitous and impersonal.

Pierce was starting to… twitch every time Hal stopped at midthigh or his glutes. The rubdown felt incomplete, he sulked to himself.

He didn't even want to admit to the vague ache of arousal that plagued him when they sat and ate lunch or dinner in front of the television. He tried to justify it to himself. He and Cynthia hadn't been having sex before the accident—it had been a while.

Hal was cute—by anybody's standards—and he'd been kind and generous with his time.

He was entertaining—he kept up a constant stream of snark and banter when they were together, and after that moment in the café, he'd kept it light—stupid things that occupied their time and made them smile but didn't tap too deeply into the heart muscle.

He had good hands, Pierce thought. Good, long-fingered, competent hands that worked deeply into his calf or his thigh or his instep or bicep or forearm, and he could take care of every sore part of Pierce's body.

Even his psyche.

Even his heart.

That was it.

It was his hands.

Right.

The next "light" workout day, they put off Christmas shopping again and went grocery shopping. Pierce insisted on paying, buying enough groceries for both of them since Hal seemed to be staying more at Pierce's place than his own.

Pierce hadn't even seen Hal's condo. For one thing, it was on the top floor, and that was a pain in the—literal—ass. All he really knew about the place was that it must have an amazing assortment of clothes, because Hal wore something different every day.

The day after grocery shopping, Pierce doubled down after his workout and proclaimed it laundry day.

Hal helped him pull the linens off the bed, neither of them mentioning that he'd been sleeping on the far end, only returning to his place to work out and shower in the morning before Pierce's time in the pool. After the load started, Pierce turned to him.

"So, go up to your place and get a load of undies or something. We'll put it in next." He knew Hal had his own washing machine—he must, because the unit above Pierce's place did laundry almost constantly, it sounded like.

Hal cocked his head, and for a moment Pierce expected him to say "Naw—I'll go run a load upstairs," which was way more logical.

Instead he looked Pierce in the eye and said, "Okay. I'll bring my toiletries here too, and some clothes."

For a moment it felt like a dare. "If you want to, why not?"

Hal's usually expressive face closed down, like he was playing poker and Pierce had just made an unexpected bet.

"Won't you be afraid someone will think the worst?"

Pierce blinked. "What's the worst?" he asked stupidly.

Hal's jaw dropped. "That we're, uh…."

Oh. Heat—sticky, sweaty heat that had become closer and closer to Pierce's skin in the past week—suddenly washed his face, his neck, his back.

"Why—" he squeaked and then cleared his throat. "It doesn't matter to me," he said, wishing he could move from the hallway, grab a soda from the fridge, a glass of water, anything. His throat felt like baby powder, the old-fashioned talcum kind with extra grit. "You're a friend. Lots of people stay in a beach house with friends."

Hal's expression opened, and what Pierce saw didn't reassure him in the least. He looked… sly and vaguely predatory. He raised his hand and feathered his fingertips across Pierce's scarred cheekbone. "Sure, Pierce. You and me, we're friends."

Pierce closed his eyes and wished….

For what?

A palm on his cheek? Hal's breath against his face?

A simple kiss?

When Pierce opened his eyes, Hal had stepped back, smiling cockily. "I'll go get the next load of laundry," he said, practically whistling. "We can go for a walk after we shove this one in the dryer."

"Wait—didn't I just work out?" Pierce demanded, although, in fact, he felt better, looser, and more mobile than he had a week and a half earlier. He had to admit, the rubber mats were a simple solution to walking on the tile, and the office chair helped him not wreck his back when he communicated with what appeared to be an office behind an exciting and lucrative job offer.

Hal paused and turned his head, winking. "Just ten minutes, my man. It won't kill you, and geez—aren't you a little interested in seeing the ocean?"

His words hit Pierce in the guilt center. "I love the ocean," he said wistfully. The ocean was one of those places in Sacramento people claimed they loved but never went to visit. Here he'd been staying, the ocean just out his back window, and he hadn't so much as opened up the sliding glass door.

"Yeah, well, we better go take it in now, you know, because the next two days we're supposed to have rain."

Pierce frowned. "I thought hurricane season was over?" Because people from Sacramento also were afraid of pretty much every type of weather—rain, snow, drought—it was all frightening.

"Well, yeah—this is just a storm. You know, raindrops? It'll be fine. Besides—why do you think the window is built with those serious blinds?" He winked. "What's the matter—think we'll be locked in here while the world ends and I'll be the only person you'll have to fuck?"

Pierce rolled his eyes and prayed the sudden zoom of his heart rate didn't show. "You're all talk," he said, trying hard to be casual. "If you need to get laid before the apocalypse, I'm pretty sure all you have to do is open your door and you'll have a line down the staircase and wrapping around the condo."

Hal's sudden sucking-a-lemon expression told him the conversation didn't take quite the turn he'd expected. "If I wanted to fuck those losers, I wouldn't be moving my toothbrush down here.

Now please tell me you have tennis shoes and not flip-flops, 'cause those things are good to get out to the pool but they're crap in the sand if you're injured."

Pierce nodded, trying hard not to think of the implications of things like loads of laundry and toothbrushes. "I can do that."

Hal nodded like it was a done deal, but as soon as he'd left the condo and shut the door behind him, Pierce limped back to his suitcase, pulled his long-neglected tennis shoes out as well as his socks, and positioned himself on the bed to try to put them both on.

The socks were… difficult. He had to hold a sock in one hand so he could balance himself against the bed, then slip a toe in before grabbing the elastic with the other hand and pulling it on. By the time he'd done that twice, he was sweating a little and feeling sore and stupid.

How—oh how—could he have fooled himself into thinking that his body was 100 percent? When he'd gotten there, he'd been at 40 percent at the most—that sort of pain, stiffness, and muscle loss didn't reappear in a day!

Or a week.

By the time Hal got back with the laundry, Pierce was sitting on the bed and staring at his feet. Yes, he'd slipped the tennis shoes on—but tying them was going to be a challenge.

"Oh, there you are," Hal said, poking his head in. "I set the basket on top of the washer so we don't forget to keep the parade moving. How are you—oh!" And God, he sounded so natural. "Would you like some help?"

"Augh!" Pierce voiced, because the frustration had been breaking him into a sweat for the last ten minutes. "How do you stand me? I'm worthless! I can't even put on my shoes!"

Hal paused on his way into the room. "There's got to be a Shakespeare quote in there," he said, like he was thinking about it hard. "About how a man's worth is more than his ability to lace his boots. Now you sound like you're in asshole mood—you're not going to kick me in the face if I squat down to tie those, are you?"

"No," Pierce told him—but sulkily. "I try not to hurt the people who help me. Usually."

"So that means there's some danger," Hal said, just to make sure. "That's good to know. You can protect yourself if you know the dangers."

Everything in Pierce's brain backed up and fountained out his ears. "You can't," he said fervently, because this suddenly seemed important. "You can't. A relationship isn't like that—you can't protect yourself, even if you know the dangers. You protect yourself and you'll just... it's like a circuit. You can't make a circuit with the vinyl still on the wires. You either strip the protection off to make the circuit complete and hope it doesn't explode, or nothing ever happens."

Hal paused, kneeling at his feet, his hands warm on Pierce's calf. "That's... well, off topic, actually. And I'd love to know where it came from. But for right now, I just need to know if you're going to kick me in the face."

He rubbed Pierce's calf absentmindedly, his hands warm and strong and capable. The taut panic wire that had been zinging up Pierce's spine since he'd realized that no, he couldn't really bend far enough to put on his shoes yet, and how embarrassing that was when this young, attractive man was... was putting himself at close range—that panic wire stilled, muted, the charge of embarrassment dampening until Pierce could breathe again.

"No," Pierce whispered huskily. "Wouldn't dream of it."

Hal blinked a couple of times, looking up at him. "How do you strip the wires?" he asked, the absentminded rubbing turning into a caress.

The question made Pierce's eyes burn. "I have no idea."

The corners of Hal's mouth turned down, and he stopped touching Pierce and made quick work of the laces. "We'll figure it out," he promised. He stood, offering Pierce a hand up, and Pierce took it, then accepted the hated cane so he could make his way through the house.

Once he got outside, the cold and humid breeze took his breath away. He kept walking, expecting Hal to catch up at any moment, but he was surprised when he'd gone nearly a hundred yards before Hal trotted up to his side. Hal zipped up a windbreaker of his own before handing Pierce a zippered hoodie.

"It's frickin' cold out here!" he called, and Pierce grimaced.

"You guys are a little spoiled," he said through the wind. He remembered going running in the chill of a Sacramento winter, when it got down to the thirties.

"Yeah, well, humor me." Hal stood solicitously and helped him on with the hoodie; then together they soldiered through the loose sand that formed a pathway through the rushes toward the harder sand of the beach. Hal's hand hovered under his elbow for a few steps, and Pierce, eschewing his pride for once, paused and took his hand, putting it firmly under his arm.

"People will think we're a couple," Hal said, and he had to talk over the sound of the surf, so it was hard to know if he was flirting or embarrassed.

"I don't mind if you don't."

Hal squeezed his elbow in response, and they hit the harder-packed sand of the beach proper.

Pierce swung toward the pounding surf and paused. The waves were decent-sized but still small compared to high tide in Monterey or Half-Moon Bay, and the horizon tinted toward gold instead of gray-blue.

But still, it was a great unfathomable deep, and since he'd hauled his limping ass out here, he wanted a good look at it.

"Why are you stopping?" Hal tugged on him, and Pierce bit his lip, standing still.

"Because," he said, having trouble raising his voice. "It deserves our respect, don't you think? If you don't respect the ocean, or time, or fate, or the big things in the world, you sort of have it coming when they knock you on your ass."

Hal stopped tugging and drew up even with him. Shyly, with tentative little pauses and jerks, he put his arm around Pierce's shoulders.

Pierce let him.

"Does it make you feel alone?" he asked, voice throbbing with a loneliness he rarely showed but Pierce had guessed at.

"Yeah," Pierce said, wrapping his arm around Hal's waist. Comfort, right?

Maybe.

"Then why do we keep coming here?"

"Because it's great and vast and holy," Pierce told him, unexpectedly moved by having it right there, in front of him, when he'd ignored it for the better part of two weeks. "And it lets us touch our toes to its surf and play."

"Do you think you'll ever be able to strip the vinyl off?" Hal asked quietly. "Let your wires touch?"

Pierce swallowed, although the question wasn't unanticipated.

"I have to know I'm strong enough to take the charge," he answered. Oh, he liked this metaphor. It was another layer of vinyl between him and the pain of the divorce, and his bitterness, and of loving someone enough for the love to hurt.

"I'll test it gently," Hal whispered. "When you're ready."

Eventually they turned and took off to the north, letting the wind and the late-afternoon shadows batter at them. They walked carefully, dodging the big bits of broken shells that were sharp enough to cut through old tennis shoes if the traveler were unwary. When Pierce's leg began to complain loudly instead of nag subtly, he turned around and let Hal escort him home.

Pierce was older, and supposedly cynical and bitter, but he found himself clinging to the younger man's promise for the rest of the walk, even through the steady rain at the end. They returned to finish the laundry and remake the bed, talking quietly under the sound of the rain driving against the sliding glass door and the roar of the pounding surf. It made Pierce feel small, like the brightly lit condo was a quiet fortress of possibility against the bleak elements, and that feeling of intimacy lasted long into a quiet evening of eggs and chips for dinner before giggling their way through *Bob's Burgers*.

For once, Pierce didn't fall asleep on the couch. At eleven o'clock he stood and stretched and reached for his cane. Hal stood at the same time and turned off the television.

"I'll turn off the lights," he offered, yawning. He blinked and looked quietly at Pierce. "If you, I don't know, wanted to roll a little closer to the center of the bed tonight, I wouldn't grab your ass or anything."

Pierce smiled. "I never thought you would."

The wind gusted hard against the glass and they shared a look, haunted, searching for protection and companionship.

Two people under the covers—maybe tonight they'd be close enough to share warmth.

Pierce had just slid into bed and was setting his phone in the charger when it buzzed.

"You have friends?" Hal joked, although he'd seen Pierce take brief texts from his sister, checking in every day to make sure he wasn't dead.

"Apparently not," Pierce said grimly. "It's Cynthia."

"Does she not know about the time change?" Hal eyed the phone with distaste—it was after eleven.

"Nope," Pierce said cheerfully. On that thought, he hit Connect and yawned directly into the phone. "Evening"—yawn—"Cynthia. Nice of you to call."

"You're not in bed yet. You don't go to bed before twelve," she said flatly over the speaker.

"I'm still recovering," Pierce told her, stung. "And I was just going to bed after a rather busy day for me. Can I help you?"

He heard her blow out a breath, which was usually her cue for remembering the social niceties. He hadn't been kidding when he'd told Hal she needed a checklist. He used to think it was her way of making sure she didn't offend anybody. It hadn't been until this last year that he'd realized she'd used the checklist in the same way zealots bombing other countries used the dogma of their faith—as a crutch to support her hypothesis that she wasn't a bad person.

"I apologize," she said civilly. "You're right. There's a time difference, and I was thoughtless."

He skipped the part where he said "That's okay" because it wasn't. "What can I do for you?" he asked politely.

"Did you file for divorce already?" she asked.

"I've been in the hospital or Florida," he said, stomach sinking. "Remember, Cynthia? The hospital? I was wrapped in bandages, and you said, 'Pierce, I forgive you.'"

"And you said you wanted a divorce. I still don't understand." Her voice lowered, and the brittle exoskeleton of bitch grew a little softer. "I don't understand why that was the final straw. You never did explain it to me."

Pierce sighed, part of him wanting to claim the easy way out and pretend exhaustion, but part of him knowing that he was ending a seven-year relationship, and he owed her better than that.

"Cynthia, what did my sister ever do to you?"

"Your sister? I don't know—nothing, I guess. What does she have to do with this?"

"You kept saying she deserved to be poor, deserved to not get nice things, deserved to have to work when her husband had a good job. She'd earned that, you said. All the time. 'Welp, if Sasha didn't want to struggle, you know what she should have done.'"

"Well, she got knocked up, Pierce—you know that—"

"Yeah, but she's a good mother. She's kind. She's a better sister than I've ever deserved. Why doesn't she deserve a good life? Why does every struggle she has have to be… some sort of bill God hands her for a mistake she made a million years ago when she was a stupid kid? When does that term of service end?"

"Pierce, I don't know what this has to do with us—"

"Everything," he said quietly, pretty sure she would never get it. "What if I made a mistake? What if I invested in the wrong thing or trusted the wrong accountant? How long would I hear about that? What if someday I vote for the wrong politician and he screws up the world? Do I ever get to fix that with you? Because marriage is based on trust, sweetheart—and I finally got to the point where I couldn't trust you to forgive me if I so much as bought the wrong pair of tennis shoes."

"But… but I never said any of those things about you," she said, her voice wobbling.

"Yeah. But you said them about somebody. Somebody I cared for. And when I tried to explain it, all you could tell me was that she should have known better. Everybody makes mistakes, hon. Everybody. Holding a mistake like that against somebody—it makes you not a very good person, that's all."

"That's all?" she asked, and it wasn't his imagination. He'd hurt her. Deeply. He hadn't thought it was possible—but then, until these last two weeks, talking to Hal until he became another chamber of Pierce's heart, he hadn't found the words.

"Maybe it was just that way for me," he soothed. "Maybe somewhere out there is someone who will take the same sort of joy you do in finding that line in the sand."

"You're judging me, you bastard!" She was trying to pull her bitch on again, but he'd left her crying, and he hated that.

"You're right." Unwelcome and unbidden, he remembered when he'd first seen her. She'd been tall, healthy—a broad-cheekboned face and thick dark hair and eyes, with the sort of smile that sparkled. "I'm sorry," he said, his voice choking. "I am. I couldn't deal with it anymore. I should probably have been gentler about it, but… but you were there. I almost died. And when I woke up, I thought, 'Right now, we can say we're sorry, and we can make it better. I don't want to live like this anymore.'"

"And I said…." She breathed deeply, obviously trying to control her own tears. "I'm sorry, Pierce," she whispered after a few hard breaths. "I'm… I still don't get it all. But I'm starting to see I fucked up."

"I should have found better words." He hauled in a big lungful of air. "But my body hurt and my heart hurt and…."

"And you didn't trust me not to hurt you again," she whispered. "Okay. Okay. This isn't what I called for, but okay."

Pierce wiped his face with his palm, and Hal reached over to his side of the bed and grabbed a few tissues, handing them to him while he pulled himself together.

"What did you call for?" he asked after one of the worst moments of his life—including when the fire department had to use the jaws of life to peel him out of his destroyed pickup truck.

"I… I was going to file the papers," she whispered. "I just wanted to make sure they hadn't been filed yet."

"You do that," he said. "I won't stop you. Send them to my sister's house. I'm coming home in January. We can be divorced by the early part of next year."

"I… I was… I found somebody," she said, half laughing. "I didn't expect to, so soon. I was hoping for a June wedding."

Pierce paused, waiting for the impact, but he was apparently in the right position, because the blow flew right by. "I'm glad," he said, meaning it. "I am sincerely glad you found someone. I… I never wished you ill."

"Pierce?" she asked, her voice aching. "Why didn't you ever ask to have children? I… I want them. I didn't realize how much until I… I met this other guy. Why not us?"

Pierce thought about it. Hal grabbed the box of Kleenex and scooted close. Closer. Until their hips and thighs were touching under the covers. Part of Pierce was distracted by the warmth of the body— of Hal's body. But most of him was still putting this part of his past to bed.

"I was afraid to ask you," he said, his heart aching too. "You… you were so mean to Sasha, Cynthia. I… I was afraid you'd judge me too."

Her voice caught in a sob. "I… I'm sorry. I'm so sorry."

And now he could say this with a clear heart. "Me too. I'm so sorry. I… this was not how I saw us."

He'd imagined them once having children, being the kind of parents he saw Sasha and Marshall being. He hadn't realized, day after day, week after week, the fear of what she'd say, what she'd do—how that had built into a shell around his heart.

"Me neither. I… I filled the paperwork out already. You've got the house, like I promised. I hired a gardener to keep up the outside. Call me before you get home. I'll have someone come in and freshen the place up." Her voice stabilized, now that she was being practical. She'd always been good with details. "I took the bed, so if you send me a link to one, I'll order the replacement and be there when it's delivered."

"That's kind. You don't have to—"

"I do." A deep shuddery breath. "I… I guess I don't have as much kindness in me as I always thought. I should probably practice before I screw up another relationship, right?"

"It took two," Pierce admitted. "I… I should have found better words."

"It… you accused me. That's what it felt like," she confessed. "I…. God. Why didn't we have this talk years ago?"

Work. Promotions. Parties. Trips. Every moment, Pierce thinking they could work through it, he could live with her another week, another month, because he loved her, right?

Until all that resentment smothered the love. Dead. No resuscitation, no more love.

"I'm sorry. Just… so sorry."

"I still care for you," she said softly. "But… but we're better off over, aren't we."

It wasn't a question. "Yeah."

"I'll send the papers to Sasha's. I… I need you to know, I never wished her ill either."

No. She hadn't. "I know."

"Take care. I'll…. Can you call me on New Year's Eve? I… I'm going to miss you, okay?"

New Year's had always been them, alone, in a cabin in Tahoe. It had been special. "Yeah," he said on a sigh. "I'll call you."

The line went dead, and Pierce fumbled the phone into the charger. *God.* Hal was there. Their bodies were touching, and Hal had heard everyth—

"What's this?" Pierce asked softly, because he had a sudden armload of Hal, weeping softly on his T-shirted chest. "Oh, baby…. Hal… what's wrong?"

"You were really nice to her," Hal sobbed. "So nice." The rest of it was lost as Pierce wrapped his arms around Hal's shaking body, but Pierce heard the word "unicorn" in there somewhere.

He reached to turn off the light, wincing a little because it had been an active day for him, and his body had stiffened up. In the darkness, Hal seemed bigger somehow, warmth and weight, collapsed against Pierce's chest.

Pierce wrapped his arms around Hal's shoulders and rocked him, keeping him safe from the storm outside and whatever raged within.

They fell asleep tangled, Pierce curled around Hal, Hal's head pressed against his chest.

Pierce dreamed about a sunny day and Hal, dressed in a white linen shirt and dark cotton trousers, offering him a flower and a kiss, in an almost perfect world.

Stripping the Vinyl

PIERCE GOT up in the middle of the night to pee, like he usually did, untangling himself gently from Hal, who slept like the dead—or an exhausted child.

He crawled back into bed, and Hal burrowed up against him again, tangling their legs and scooting down so he could rest his cheek against Pierce's chest. Pierce, drowsy and uninhibited, stroked his back gently.

A warm human being in his bed. The joy of that event staggered him.

What're you doing, Pierce? You leave in two and a half weeks!

Leave? Not see this absurdly pretty kid day after day? Not have Hal urging him unmercifully in the pool and chattering about Looney Tunes and *Bob's Burgers* in the meantime?

Unconsciously, Pierce tightened his arms around Hal's shoulders. He fell asleep dreaming of a giant hole in his house at home and how nobody seemed to notice that if you walked into the bedroom, you'd fall into an enormous black pit without boundaries or bottom.

When the dark was still fathomless, he woke up to feel somebody—Hal—moving his lips down his bare stomach.

Pierce grunted and pulled at his shirt—it seemed to have rucked up in the night—and Hal gently but firmly pushed the shirt back up. His lips kept traveling down, down, then up, spending a moment on Pierce's nipples, until the haze of sleep and arousal made him groan.

Words... Pierce had to make words....

Words like... ah, God, hands everywhere... nipples... nibble just... oh, nip? Lick? Suck... no, no, different words.

No words?

Should there be "no" words here?

"Hal...," he whispered, raising his hands to Hal's thick hair to maybe pull him off... or knead his fingers in it, silky, and massage fingertips against Hal's scalp.

Hal pulled up long enough to say "Shh…." and hold his fingertips against Pierce's lips.

Okay. Hush. That was the only word.

Pierce closed his eyes against the darkness, seeing the pressure and pleasure of his body as bright white clouds against his eyelids.

A cloud at one nipple, under the play of Hal's tongue, and then at the other. Hal skimmed his fingers through the decently thick patch of hair on Pierce's chest, and Pierce breathed deeply and arched his hips, trying not to flail, trying to decide if he was dreaming.

The strobes of light danced behind his eyes. Bongo drumbeats of visual sensation, nipples, played to explosions of light, soft thrums of caress, down his ribs, across his soft stomach.

A hesitation at the waistband of his shorts, a flicker of lights as they were dragged down.

More tickling lights along his shaft, and a wafting pulse of breath along the head.

Pierce moaned, the actual sound in the quiet of the storm shocking.

"Hush," Hal breathed, and that one word anchored him in the present.

The rest was sensual stimuli, his harsh breathing overshadowing the rain beating on the windows and that watercolor firework behind his closed eyes.

Rough tongue, wet heat, a hot cave of pressure—Pierce sighed loudly, afraid to make more noise, afraid that if he even blinked, the moment would disappear. He threw his arm over his eyes and arched into Hal's mouth, his breathy moans growing but not breaking the bubble of silence over two men on the bed in the dark room.

He lost himself in the wonder of his body, the same body that had felt mostly useless, a betrayal of flesh and blood, over the past five months.

His body did amazing things.

Sure hands tugged gently on his balls, and that was it. "Coming," he managed, but the heat and the pressure didn't let up.

I should say something. About being HIV negative.

But he was coming, ejaculating, that part of his body working with amazing coordination considering it hadn't been used in more than half a year.

He came forever, until he felt pumped from the inside out, collapsing on the bed and pushing feebly at Hal's head when he became oversensitized.

"I... uh... neg—"

Hal covered his mouth with a sloppy, spit-covered hand. "Hush...."

Pierce moaned, his eyes closed of their own volition. Tired. So tired. Wrung out by emotion, by exertion, by oh-my-God sex! He curled into a ball on his side, only peripherally aware that someone was wiping at his groin with Kleenex and pulling his sleep pants and underwear up over his hips.

The rustling around his body stopped, and Hal backed carefully up against his front. Pierce flung his arm over that slim, taut waist and pulled closer, until they were spooning.

Warm and safe, content in a way he didn't know he could be, he fell asleep.

When he woke up in the morning, Hal was toasting bagels in the kitchen, singing Barry Manilow to himself. Until Pierce went to the bathroom and tried to peel his underwear off his come-sticky pubic hair, he thought the whole thing had been a dream.

"It's still raining and thundering!" Hal called from the living room. "You may as well shower—no pool today."

"Bummer," he muttered. The cleansing of the pool—that felt like something he needed right then.

"I'll give you a yoga lesson and a rubdown," Hal said, his voice coming right from the door. "So don't hop in the shower just yet, 'cause yoga will make you sweat."

"Okay—should I stay in my sleep pants?"

"Those'll work fine. Now hurry up and eat—I need to work you out so we can go shopping today."

Oh yeah. "Christmas shopping," Pierce said, the thought actually comforting him. Christmas. His family. His plans. Things not derailed by what may or may not have happened in the heart of the night. "You want we should get decorations? I mean, I'm not leaving until Christmas Eve. Some tinsel might be nice."

The breathing on the other side of the bathroom door grew awfully damned still. "Sure. Yeah. Let's do that. It'll be the only Christmas I get."

Pierce sucked in a breath full of mostly razor blades, and Hal padded back to the kitchen.

By himself?

Pierce would leave and Hal would be here by himself?

Because it's perfectly sane to ask this guy you've known for two weeks to come with you.

Alone?

Pierce may have only known the guy for two weeks, but he was pretty sure Hal hated to be alone.

But what sort of asshole asked a guy he barely knew to drop his life in Florida and come to Sacramento on a whim?

Pierce washed his hands and padded on the new rubber mats into the kitchen, where Hal had dished up two bagel sandwiches with some orange juice.

"This is awesome," he said, heart giving a big throb in his chest. "You're... you're really good at taking care of me."

Hal grinned sunnily. "See, that's excellent to hear, because my parents think I can barely take care of myself."

"They're deluded," Pierce said shortly, sitting down and unfolding his paper napkin onto his lap. "They've never woken up to bagels and orange juice with you."

He expected Hal to add "And blowjobs!" and maybe broach the subject—but that didn't happen.

"Well, maybe they were never as kind as you were," Hal said, smiling shyly.

Pierce's stomach knotted. "Kind?" God, that's what he'd said the day before too, after Pierce had gotten off the phone with his ex-wife.

"Yeah. The way you talked to Cynthia—that was... I mean, I was prepared to hear you hate her. I thought she sounded like a real bitch—but you didn't. You were... kind. And in the end, I think she got it. She got why the divorce. She understood."

Pierce looked away, feeling uncomfortable. "I'm not always nice," he said, suddenly desperately afraid of letting Hal down. "You know that. I was a grumpy bastard two weeks ago."

"You were in pain," Hal said simply. He beamed up at Pierce, showing no regret about the things they'd done in the night—hell, almost no knowledge of it. Just simple, uplifting forgiveness.

Pierce nodded and tried to give Hal something real. "Less pain every day," he said brightly.

"That's what I like to hear." Hal wiped his face and nodded decisively. "Okay—I'm going to go get my yoga mats and an area rug from upstairs—I don't want you trying yoga on the tile."

"I could do yoga in your place," Pierce said, and Hal's furtive look from under his lashes made something in Pierce's stomach twist.

"I, uh, need to clean up there," Hal told him. "It's just easier for me to go get my stuff."

Pierce nodded, wondering again what sort of damage Hal could have inflicted on his apartment in the two days after Thanksgiving and before he'd come down to the pool and seen Pierce struggling to do water aerobics to his iPhone.

In a dim, sort of distant way, it was starting to dawn on him that Hal had been very much alone in his life before he'd sprawled in a lounge chair and started bossing Pierce around.

Hal deserved more than that.

"So," Pierce said, resolving to talk about the blowjob in the room. "About—"

"Christmas shopping? I figure Target for decorations and toys, you think? And you should be able to get an appliance there for your sister, right?"

The desperation in his voice hit the raw edge of Pierce's nerve, and Pierce finally got it. They weren't supposed to talk about the blowjob in the night.

And for a moment he struggled against that—because he wanted to talk about it. Hell, he wanted to reciprocate it. But, oh God. He was leaving in two weeks. Whatever happened in those spare, breathless moments in the dark, how much could it mean?

Everything, you fucking coward. It means everything.

But Pierce had been locked in the silence of his own head since…
well, not even before the accident. Since before Cynthia, really.

Since Loren.

Since he'd last believed in unicorns.

"What, uh," Pierce struggled to articulate. "What, uh, would
you like for Christmas?"

Hal's full mouth—*had been wrapped around Pierce's cock*—
quirked up at the corners. "A teddy bear," he said with satisfaction.
"Something… something furry. To hug in bed."

Pierce remembered Hal's fingers petting the silky hair on his
chest as he sucked on Pierce's nipples. "I can do bears," he said, fully
aware of the innuendo and unable to stop it.

"You can do otters too," Hal said with a wink. "But I really only
want a bear."

Pierce blushed and took a big bite of his bagel. "Mm'kay," he
said through a full mouth. "'M brrrr."

Hal burst out laughing, and they finished breakfast in peace.

AN HOUR later, Pierce was stretching awkwardly, trying to attain the
warrior's pose, and Hal was grabbing his sweaty body everywhere at
once to help him find the position.

"Ouch!" Pierce complained after a particularly hard crank to
his knee.

"Oh shit—I'm sorry! Okay, you know what? You work so hard
in the water, you had me fooled. I'm going to go back to very basic
moves—like kids' moves. They'll be good for your coordination, and
if we increase the speed, they'll help you with cardio. You game?"

Pierce's body hurt—a lot—and those warm fuzzy thoughts he'd
had about Hal that morning had become sort of thin and meshy over
the last fifteen minutes.

"Yeah," he admitted, pulling his feet under him and putting his
hand out to try to find balance. Hal caught his hand and pulled up
behind his elbow. "This isn't working."

"Okay. I'm going to help you sit down, and I need you to spread
your legs. Let's start there."

Pierce let himself be stretched and wondered again who had told this kid he couldn't make a living doing what he was doing. Yeah, sure—he made mistakes. But no teacher started out perfect. And Hal had such a good heart, such a willingness to try what he needed in order to make his plan work.

How could you say no in the face of that raw enthusiasm?

Pierce obviously couldn't.

But the thing was, when he said something funny and Hal turned those laughing brown eyes on Pierce's face, Pierce didn't ever want to try. He wanted to tell Hal yes to absolutely everything, anything, as long as he could make this young man that happy.

And as Hal squatted at his feet and pushed his toes toward his nose to help with his dorsiflex, Pierce was finding fewer and fewer reasons he shouldn't do that.

Hal was honest about the workout being more intense than he'd anticipated—so he kept it to forty-five minutes and did lots of therapeutic breathing at the end. Pierce was grateful—and even more grateful that at the end he felt refreshed and not destroyed.

And then Hal helped Pierce stand up, and they were standing chest to chest, with only the memory of the hallucinogenic midnight blowjob between them.

"I'm negative," Pierce blurted.

Hal raised his eyebrows and smirked. "Yeah, but we're working on that." He said it with a little shake of the head, and Pierce heard the *Please, please don't talk about it* in that movement and took a deep breath.

"Forewarned is forearmed," he said, letting that have two meanings.

Hal's eyes widened for a moment, as though the thought surprised him. "Very true. And I've now been warned of your negativity."

He gestured grandly then, breaking the heat between them, and Pierce hobbled to the shower.

The rest of the day seemed to be spent in that dual state of awareness, though. On the one hand, they were the two guys who had spoken frankly and slyly for the last two weeks.

On the other hand, every time they touched, whether it was when Hal offered him a hand out of the car or bumped his shoulder as Pierce leaned his weight on the shopping cart, was like shaking a bottle full of lightning.

Sparks everywhere.

"Hm… throw pillows, what do you think?" Hal asked, looking at some brightly colored Christmas pillows with trees and holly berries on them.

"I think Derrick will be surprised," Pierce said, and then, remembering that Derrick and Miranda were supposed to be there on New Year's Day, said, "Throw them in, with some of the dark blue too. It'll be like a thank-you gift."

"That's really nice!" Hal said, with that surprising excitement for "niceness." "Also, it's really convenient, since we can use them too!"

"Well, if Derrick didn't like gifts that served double duty, he wouldn't have gotten me a PS4 with three extra controllers last year," Pierce told him dryly.

For a moment Hal looked blank, and then it hit him. "So he could play at your house," he said, nodding in approval. "But why three extras?"

"For our wives." Pierce shrugged. "Miranda liked to play but Cynthia didn't, so Miranda, being a better person than any of the rest of us hosers, pretended not to want to play so Derrick and I could have the game room to ourselves and she and Cynthia could go buy decorating stuff at Target."

"Hm…." Hal glared at the throw pillows like they were responsible for irony. "I am not sure how to feel about any of that. I mean, on the one hand, Derrick sounds like my kind of guy—"

"You'll love him," Pierce said, thinking that Derrick and Miranda could… could look after Hal, after they got there. "He's, like, ultra-super cool."

"Describe ultra-super cool," Hal said, eyebrow cocked skeptically.

Well. Here was an embarrassing story. "Like, he walked in on me and Loren before he knew about the bi thing. Took one look at Loren on his knees—"

"Oh my God!"

"Yeah—embarrassing, right?"

It could have been. It could have been horrific. But Derrick really was the best.

"What did you do?" Hal asked, entranced.

"It was more like what did *he* do. And what he did was take one look at Loren there and said, 'Oh my God, you're bi!'" Pierce ignored Hal's bark of laughter and continued. "And I said, 'Is this a problem?'" And Pierce left out how terrified he was, because he and Derrick... well, inseparable since grade school, which was why they'd roomed together in college. "And he said, 'It is when you don't leave a sock on the bedroom door, asshole! I don't care who you're with, I'll never unsee you having sex!'"

Hal laughed, ducking his head and then looking back at him with a softly bitten lip. "Poor man," he said, but his apple cheeks were popping with the force of his grin.

"Yeah. I'd be worried it scarred him for life, but he met Miranda about a month after that, and suddenly our apartment was made of socks on the door, so I think he'll be okay."

"That's... that's sweet." Hal's grin faded. "So they've been together since college?" he asked, suddenly uncertain. "Over ten years?"

"Yeah. Hey—this little wooden Christmas tree. Don't hate me, but I think this could go on the end table by the window, don't you?"

Hal looked at it and nodded, swallowing hard. "Yeah," he said. "It's perfect. I... I thought Russ and me were going to do that," he blurted. "Like... like your friend and his wife."

Pierce almost dropped the Christmas tree into the cart from about two feet up. He barely managed to lower it so it rested awkwardly on the throw pillows, and wondered if maybe he shouldn't have visited the kid's section first.

"Is this the guy who cheated on you?" he asked, because he knew that name now.

"Yeah." Hal's eyes cruised restlessly, and he reached out to a wooden dreidel, colored blue and white. "My mother has one of these," he said, pleased. "I... I mean, I have no idea what it's for, because we did Christmas like my dad's family, but—"

"We'll put it by the Christmas tree," Pierce told him, setting it carefully next to the tree. "Do you want a menorah?"

Hal frowned. "No... 'cause, again, I have no idea what it's for. But I do want a tinsel banner, so find that aisle, quick!"

"Yeah, sure. When did you and Russ break up?" Because Hal was avoiding two questions today, and if Pierce didn't get to, Hal didn't get to.

"Valentine's Day, this year," Hal told him, rolling his eyes. "So no, I'm not all sentimental about him now because he broke up with me before Christmas."

"Glad to know that," Pierce said dryly, and then he stopped and sighed. "Hal?"

"What?"

For a moment, they looked each other in the eyes, the bustle around them of a zillion people on a holiday mission making the painful personal moment a little easier to bear.

"If you ever want to tell me something… you know. Real. I could be that guy for you. Now. I mean, I couldn't have been that guy for you right after Thanksgiving. I was too pissed at myself. But I could be that guy for you now if you want."

A faint smile pulled the corners of Hal's mouth up.

"I'll… I'll keep that in mind." But he turned away quickly, reaching onto the shelves and coming back with an exquisite holiday star, a combination of fiber optics and plastic filigree that managed to look enchanting in spite of what should have been very tacky beginnings. "Don't hate me, but I love this."

Pierce grimaced, oddly let down. "Throw it in the cart," he said.

"But we don't have anything to put it on."

"We'll get some cord and hang it from the ceiling. It'll look avant-garde—no one will have to know we just made it up as we went along."

Hal laughed, but there was no joy in the sound. "Apparently that's all of adulthood."

"Yeah, well, adulthood has some surprisingly awesome moments, so don't knock it," Pierce snapped, trying hard not to be heartbroken. He stalked through decorations a little faster, wanting to get to the kids' department before the weariness in his legs became a problem.

Hal caught up with him easily and placed his hand on the back of Pierce's elbow. Normally Pierce didn't need this unless he was using his cane, and right before he shook off the hand, he recognized it for what it truly was:

A peace offering.

"Some dinner after we get the presents and get out of here?" Hal offered as a treaty.

"Sure. What do you want for Christmas, though?"

"I already told you—a teddy bear!"

Pierce grimaced. "Oh, dammit! Speaking of things in the kids' department—"

Hal smacked his forehead with his palm. "Yeah. You have short people to spoil. Where to, hoss?"

God, Target was huge. Past the linens and a rockin' discussion of whether it was okay to have lavender-scented dreams when you slept on purple sheets, and on through towels, with more arguments about whether pretty patterned towels meant someone was douchey—Hal said yes—or just Californian—Pierce was on that boat.

Finally, just before Hal came to the conclusion that all Californians were inevitably douchey—which Pierce would have argued against to the death—they found the toy department.

And Nirvana.

"Oh. My. God." Hal swung around the Lego shelves like Julie Andrews did a helicopter twirl on a mountain in the alps. "Legos? Seriously? This is what Legos look like these days?"

Pierce looked around, comforted by the fact that he was pretty sure Darius only had about half these sets. "What? You never got Legos as a kid?"

He got a scowl in return. "My cutoff date for Legos was twelve. Some asshole put a little number on the box that said they were good from eight to twelve, so my dad the judge and mom the helicopter parent started getting me foreign language lessons and science camp memberships after that."

"You know, you're not making a case for money making a good parent," Pierce said, truly dismayed. "Do you *see* the Millennium Falcon? That thing's good 'til you're sixteen!"

Hal smirked at him. "How old were you?"

"Well, Sasha and Marshall gave it to me three years ago— remember that study I'm crazy about? It's got a Lego Millennium

Falcon in a glass case on the shelf. Took Derrick and me three days, but man, it was worth it."

"So, what? You and your sister just swap Lego sets?" Hal picked up a giant Lego Batman scenario that cost a hundred dollars easy.

"You forget," Pierce said patiently. "My parents were douchebags too. So basically, all *we* got for Christmas was Sunday school clothes and Bible study coloring books—"

"Yuck!"

"I'm saying. We got older, and it was mostly wooden chess sets for me and sewing kits for Sasha. So when I was twelve, and we could walk to the store together, we would save our allowance and buy each *other* gifts. She always bought me Legos, because—dude? Can you see?"

"I'm sold," Hal said seriously, grabbing a big bucket of assorted parts and looking at it with lust in his eyes.

"Well, I would buy her Barbies. And now that Abigail is, like, four years old, I promised Sasha I'd keep that kid eyeballs-deep in Barbie dolls and Monster High and whatever else is current and pink and awesome." Pierce gestured grandly. "If she wants Legos, I'll get them. Pink Legos? I'm on it. Those kids are getting more toys than they know what to do with—Sasha and I made a pact."

"Word," Hal said, nodding like he was now the choir and Pierce could preach. "But, about this bucket of Legos—don't you think we could make an awesome Christmas tree with this?"

"Put it in," Pierce said, liking this plan. "And grab the giant *Guardians of the Galaxy* one behind you." He grinned, feeling magnanimous and evil. "And go find two teddy bears—one for you and one for Sasha."

"Wait—I thought you were getting your sister a Keurig?" Hal asked suspiciously.

Pierce remembered his sister as a child, all big brown eyes and dark hair, pale and afraid of pissing off Mom and Dad. "A coffee maker to wake up her inner adult," he said with dignity, "and a teddy bear to comfort her inner child."

Hal grinned. "Okay—you look at Barbies, and I'll go cruise stuffed animals. Meet back in five."

Pierce thought about family planning and wondered if he could sneak lubricant and condoms into the cart and get back in time to find Abigail's present. He cursed his range of motion, because he knew he wouldn't make it, and being... overt about it might just frighten Hal off.

Dammit.

But he owed his niece a present and had just decided on the Monster High Mansion when Hal came around the corner, one giant stuffed pink bear under one arm, and a giant stuffed bear with green eyes and light brown fur held against his chest with the other.

Pierce looked from the bear to Hal's face and back again. "Is that supposed to be me?" he asked dryly.

"Do you let me cuddle you like this?" Hal asked, waggling his eyebrows.

"I might." Pierce waggled his back, wondering how long they could flirt without actually mentioning the damned blowjob-in-the-dark-room thing that had happened the night before.

"Then yes," Hal said archly, putting both bears in the laden cart. He paused for a moment and looked at the cart again. "And we're going to have to stop debating on which bear I'm going to sleep with and check out. This thing's full and"—he raked Pierce's body over with a critical eye—"unless I miss my guess, you're getting tired."

"No I'm—" Pierce yawned. "—not."

Hal raised an eyebrow, looking bored.

"Fine. And I'm starving. Let's go."

The line was damned long, and by the time they got through it, Pierce was limping badly. Hal made him go sit down in the CR-V while he unloaded the cart, and when he got back into the car, he sighed like he'd made a big decision.

"Okay—here's what we're going to do. I'm going to call a chain restaurant for takeout, we'll go park in the takeout spot and I'll run in and get it, and we'll take it back home with us. That way you can eat and crash, and I can start immediately on making a Christmas tree out of Legos because honestly, it *is* all about me, and that sounds like the most fun *ever*."

Pierce laughed—because how could he not. "Yeah," he said, wishing he was a woman with ibuprofen in her purse or something. "That sounds awesome."

Hal's hand, warm on his shoulder, surprised him. "I'll take care of you," he said softly. "I'm young, but I can train up quick."

And Pierce, tired, confused, and in need of some reassurance, took it for what it was. "You'll do a great job," he said. "I don't know why you worry."

Hal looked away. "Yeah. Yeah, you do." He pulled out his phone and started tapping into it without looking up. "So, Applebee's—what's your favorite item there?"

Pierce ordered a sandwich, and they were both quiet on the drive. Hal parked, and Pierce leaned back against the seat, eyes closed.

"It'll be a minute," Hal said softly. "I'm going to run next door to get something before getting our food."

Pierce kept his eyes closed and nodded. He wasn't even sure when Hal came out, takeout bags rustling as he put them behind the driver seat, and he tried hard not to drool on the way home.

HE WOKE up for takeout at Derrick's little glass-topped table, the Target bags sitting accusingly in the corner of the room.

"We forgot wrapping paper," Pierce said, halfway through his sandwich, and Hal smacked his forehead with his palm.

"D'oh! God, we suck at this!"

"Right?" Pierce couldn't help the shocked laughter. "We're, like, epically bad. We'll have to learn to make lists."

"Either that or set up a little minicamp at Target. 'Hello, we're the eternal shoppers. We go home between trips, but we have a cot for the times we forget half the shit we came for.'"

"That would totally work," Pierce agreed. "Like in those apocalyptic movies, where people gather in a shopping mall or Target. You've got years' worth of canned goods and all the clothes in your size you could ask for."

"And they've got video games and probably their own generator," Hal said, because maybe when you were twenty-three you remembered the important stuff.

"And sleeping bags and futons—" *And condoms and lubricant and privacy.* "—and we, uh, you could be totally comfortable there for quite some time." Oh God. Pierce had just remembered why he was the bear and why Hal would rank videogames as a postapocalyptic necessity.

But Hal didn't seem to think there was anything amiss. "We," he said, eyes to the side like he was imagining something pleasant. "*We* could be happy and comfortable for quite some time."

"Okay," Pierce mumbled, not sure what he was agreeing to. Suddenly he didn't care. "*We* could be happy and comfortable in Target after the apocalypse. It'll be our destination place when we're running from the zombie hordes."

They finished dinner, talking about the best strategy for defeating the vicious undead, and Pierce got up to help clear the table while Hal raided the bags.

"You can throw the pillows on the couch," Pierce instructed, rinsing silverware and cups. "That's where they were meant to go anyway."

Hal started to laugh, all evil. "Throw pillows. Get it? They're *throw* pillows, and I'm throwing them."

Pierce stared at him. "Oh dear God."

He repeated his evil cackle and sailed the next pillow across the room like a Frisbee. The next one went too far, and Pierce stuck his hand up and caught it before it could hit the refrigerator.

They both stopped and stared at Pierce's game hand and arm in shock.

Pierce met Hal's grinning countenance with fierce triumph of his own, and then Hal pumped his fist, dancing on the hard tile of the living room with undisguised glee.

"*I* am going to be the best massage therapist/personal trainer on the *planet*! I'm rehab therapy *king of the frickin' world*!"

Pierce dried his good hand at the sink, then grabbed the pillow to chuck it at Hal's head. Hal didn't even duck, he was enjoying his celebration too much. And why not? Pierce grinned at him, not quite ready to mambo—or so he thought.

"You don't get out of this that easy," Hal told him, dancing into the kitchen. "Here—turn toward me—conga line! You're the big spoon!"

Oh wow. Hands on slim hips, Bugs Bunny moves ready! There was only the music in Hal's head, and he slowed it down enough for Pierce to keep up. *Bum-bum-bum-bum-ba-BUMP, bum-bum-bum-bum-ba-BUMP*, together they conga-trained into the living room. Hal grabbed his hands and turned them around so Pierce's back was toward the couch, and Pierce, caught up in the madness, wrapped his arms around Hal's waist as he fell backward, pulling Hal down on top of him.

He turned at the last moment, depositing Hal sloppily next to him, while the two of them laughed like children. Then they both seemed to take a breath at the same time, and the moment grew long, stretched breathlessly between them, a taffy moment with no end.

Pierce broke first, biting his lip and looking down at Hal's chest, heat stealing over his cheeks. *Kiss me, Hal. Please.* Hal leaned forward, and Pierce looked up into his eyes. For a moment, while his heart beat in his ears, they stared at each other, and Hal's plush mouth pursed, came closer, and...

...veered to the right to gently buss Pierce's cheek.

Come on!

Hal pushed himself up to his feet, bouncing like the moment never happened.

Oh. Maybe last night was a fluke. Maybe he's just really kind and doesn't want me after all. I'm older and have scars, and I was pretty fuckin' average anyway. Maybe he just wants to be friends.

He is a pretty amazing friend.

"Are you ready to do the Lego thing?" Hal asked, and Pierce nodded bemusedly, trying hard to keep his disappointment to himself.

THEY WERE deep into the intricacies of making rectangular Legos turn into a round shape when his phone buzzed with Sasha's nightly text—and then rang, because apparently the text was a warning shot.

Pierce answered the phone saying, "Hey, Sasha, what's up?"

"You sound happier," she said, but *she* didn't, and Pierce's antennae went on high alert.

"I am. What's wrong?"

"They're coming," she said, voice crumbling. "Pierce, I didn't know what to do. They called up and said they were coming for Christmas—they didn't ask or anything. I mean, I don't even know how they knew my number. I wasn't even living here the last time I talked to them."

Pierce blinked, trying not to freak out. "Wait. You mean—our *parents* are coming?"

"Yeah. What am I going to do?"

Oh Jesus. "Do you want them in your house, Sash? Be honest. I was the bastard who told them not to talk to you at all if they couldn't be nice. If you want them back in your life—"

"No!" Her voice cracked into tears. "No. Pierce, I can't even…. My kids just watched me cry, and Marshall had to help me breathe after they hung up, and he was going to call them up and tell them to go to hell but… but he's not a… a *warrior*, Pierce. You are." And now she sounded like she was crying quietly, like when they were kids. "You are. Please, I know you're mad at yourself now, because you got mad because you were hurt. But… but that's just because you're used to being on the making-it-right side of things. That's why you and Cynthia, I think—I mean, for all her faults, Pierce, she kept trying to make the world better."

"Don't worry," he said grimly. "Sasha, don't worry. Where'd they call from?"

"I'll text you the number," she said, sniffling. "Please don't let them come to my house on Christmas. I'm sorry I'm such a… a fucking *mouse* about this—"

"Stop," he said, making sure his voice was firm. "Sasha, you are strong. You walked out of their lives and you… I was an asshole when I was there, but even *I* could see what a good life you made for your kids. So don't… don't be mad at yourself because you don't have the asshole gene, okay? I guess it's all I'm good for."

"No," she protested. "No—that's not why I asked you."

Pierce's mouth twisted—he couldn't help it. But he kept the bitterness out of his voice when he talked to his little sister. "Honey,

I'm going to go call them now, okay?" He pushed himself up off the couch, where Hal was looking at him with big eyes.

Well, Hal didn't want him at all—he might as well show Hal who he really was.

"Thank you," Sasha said on a sigh. "Thanks, Pierce. I'm so grateful."

"Love you, Sash," he said quietly. "I'll take that info now."

He disconnected and grimaced at Hal. "You don't want to hear what's going to happen next."

"You're not an asshole," Hal said staunchly.

Pierce sighed. "You're such a sweet guy. You wouldn't know an asshole if...." *He came in your mouth in the dark.* "If he threw a pillow at your head." And with that, Pierce limped to the bedroom, just as his phone dinged with Sasha's text and a number he thought would have changed by now.

He hit the link with a sigh.

"Hello, Atwater residence, Diana Atwater speaking."

Oh hell—his mother hadn't changed in the least.

"This is your son, Pierce, Diana. I've called to ask you very nicely to stay the fuck away from Florida."

"Pierce?" For once his mother sounded startled. "Pierce, why on earth would you be calling?"

"You called Sasha, right?"

"Yes, but you made it very clear that you never wished to speak to us again. We honored your wishes. Your sister, on the other hand—"

"Is the same person she was eight years ago, except happy. Why in the hell would you call her up out of the blue and fuck that up?"

He waited for something to happen inside him, something that would relent, some scrap of decency that would let him feel bad about the way he was speaking to his mother. But all he could remember was a rigid back in the front of the car as his mother taxied him and Sasha around town, six days a week, to the relentless activities that he and Sasha had been enrolled in pretty much since preschool. Derrick would get to soccer practice singing Led Zeppelin at the top of his lungs with his father or hanging out for one last bit of conversation with his mom. Pierce would slingshot the fuck out of the back seat like all the demons of hell were on his ass.

Or at least one big freezing demon with perfectly coifed hair.

"I really don't know what this has to do with you, Pierce—"

"I'm going to be at Sasha's for Christmas. Did you let her tell you that?"

There was a shocked silence. "No—we didn't think—"

"What? That Sasha and I talked? I wrecked my car, Mom. Wrecked my car, lost my job, almost died, and got a divorce. And Sasha stepped up to take care of me like I took care of her. I'm staying at a friend's beach house right now, but you know what? I *promised* to come back. And Sasha wants me back for Christmas. So I'm going to be there, and Sasha wants me there and not you. Live with that."

"But... but, Pierce." And for the first time in his life, Pierce heard his mother's voice waver. "Our grandchildren. You'd deprive... your father and me of meeting our grandchildren?"

Pierce took a deep breath and thought of forgiveness. "You really want to meet your grandchildren? Start with a card on their birthdays. Start with presents. Start with a phone call once a week where you get to know them. *Don't* call your daughter up and bully her into something she would rather not do."

"You really don't think much of us, do you?"

It was not his imagination. She sounded hurt. The last time they'd had this conversation, she'd sounded pissed and superior and smug. She'd told him that his interference would be immaterial— Sasha would come crawling back eventually.

Shit.

Just like Cynthia. Someone had fucking learned.

"No," he said, his voice dropping. "I don't. But you still have a chance with Sasha. Not this Christmas you don't. This Christmas I'm going to be there, in all my pissed-off glory—"

"We could see you too, son," his mother said hesitantly.

"I'm bisexual. I'm seeing a man right now. No."

Yeah, he'd always wondered if he should come out to his parents—why would he need to if he was married to Cynthia? If Loren was going to break up with him? His mother's harshly drawn breath was all the reward he'd ever needed.

"Why would you even tell us that?" his mother asked, her voice breaking.

"Why would it even matter?" he shot back. "See? You're the same people. You're the people who screamed at Sasha until she broke. You're the people who drove her boyfriend—the one who'd proposed, by the way—away with a baseball bat. You're the same judgmental, disapproving assholes you've always been—and you just proved it all over again. You want a relationship with your grandchildren, go ahead and send a card and some presents. Just remember, I've got an eight-year head start spoiling them rotten, and they are *always* going to love me best."

"Does Sasha even know who she's exposing her children to?" Diana asked, voice all venom. "Does *she* know about your... your... *perversion*?"

"She's known since I was in college. See, you were never really interested in us as people—but we always had each other's backs. Still do. So, are you coming to Christmas if I'm there?"

"No. I'll have to discuss this with your father to see if we want to come at all."

"Just say no. Neither of us want you back in our lives. If you can't do the work, don't bother."

It was as good an exit line as any, so he hung up. Pierce set the phone in the charger and sat heavily on the bed. He heard a noise in the doorway and turned his head, unsurprised to see Hal there.

"Sorry," he rasped, hating himself so badly in that moment.

"Why?" Hal asked. He reached behind him and switched off the hall light. Pierce realized the bedroom was the only room in the house that still had a light on. Well, it was pretty late. Suddenly wiped out, he pulled his feet out of his flip-flops and pulled his mostly clean sleep pants out from under the pillow.

"That wasn't... pleasant." Pierce sighed. "Hold on a second." He grabbed his phone off the charger and texted *I told her I'd be there and I'm bisexual. Make sure Marshall knows.*

Pierce set the phone down and wrestled with his cargo shorts. After he won, he laid them on the dresser and grabbed the sleep pants.

"You can just wear boxers," Hal said. It sounded like he was tripping over his tongue.

Pierce didn't even look at him. He felt... numb. And sad. And unwanted.

His phone pinged. *Marshall's always known. She just texted and said she'd be in touch, but they wouldn't be coming for Christmas. Thank you.*

He swallowed. God, he still couldn't look Hal in the eyes. *Love you, Sasha. Night.*

Love you back. Night.

His fingers were still fairly nimble. He'd realized that in the past two weeks—his arm had been broken and sustained muscle and nerve damage, but his hand and fingers worked just fine. He unbuttoned his overshirt and laid it down next to the cargo pants before setting the phone down one last time.

He felt Hal's weight depress the bed and stretched forward to turn off the light while the comforter under his ass got yanked down. Nice. That was a nice thing to do.

He was unprepared for Hal's heat at his back or the hands at the hem of his T-shirt in the dark.

"What are you—"

"Shh…." Hal breathed into his ear. "Just… hush."

This again?

But he could feel Hal's lips his neck, his ear, down his shoulder. *This* again didn't seem like a terrible thing. Hal lifted his T-shirt up over his head, and Pierce could raise his hands up to help him out—a thing he couldn't have done two and a half weeks ago.

"Thank—"

Hal kissed the back of his neck, and he grunted, all senses going on overdrive. Then Hal put his lips almost touching the whorls of Pierce's ear. "You are *not* an asshole."

Pierce moaned, his entire body going boneless. Hal moved and pulled him backward until he was lying face up in the darkness. He stared at the ceiling while Hal kissed his way down again, thinking *Dammit, no. Not… not… ah….*

Hal's mouth, dreamy, insistent, wrapped around Pierce's cock through the cotton of his boxers. Pierce massaged his head as Hal mouthed him. Pierce grunted, his hips bucking, his libido getting the hint that last night's activity had *not* been a fluke.

He was going to say something, give a direction, ask if he could reciprocate—*something*—but then Hal tugged at his boxers, and he was naked under the cool air of the ceiling fan, his knees spread before the world. Hal repositioned himself between Pierce's legs, and Pierce lifted his head, watching Hal suck his cock, bare now, over Pierce's long body.

Hal's eyes gleamed wickedly in the dark room, daring him to say anything. *Daring* him to actively engage.

"Harder," Pierce whispered. "Faster. Oh God, *yes!*"

Hal took him down, all the way, grabbing his shaft as he pulled his head back, and Pierce urged him on unashamedly. If this was what Hal wanted to do, Pierce wanted it—oh God, how he wanted it.

"That's so good," Pierce rasped. "So… oh God. Hal…. Hal, I'm going to…."

Then Hal slid his fingers, slick with spit, down Pierce's crease, and Pierce almost sobbed. One finger, penetrating, just a little, just enough….

"Come!" Pierce cried, tugging on his hair.

But like the night before, when Pierce had been able to pretend it never really happened, Hal sucked hard on the bell and swallowed.

"Thank you," Pierce chanted. "Thank you, thank you, thank you…."

Hal moved off his cock and pulled up his shorts, sliding up the bed to rest his head on Pierce's chest.

And Pierce wanted more. With another tug on Hal's hair, Pierce held his head back.

"Kiss me," he ordered gently.

Hal's mouth, glazed with spit and come, swollen from sucking on Pierce's cock, parted. "But—"

Pierce kissed him, the kiss as sensual as the blowjob. He fell into Hal's mouth, plundered it, tasted his own semen and swept his tongue in for more. Hal groaned, and Pierce turned his body so Hal was lying on his back in his underwear.

Oh Lord—he was so beautiful. Cut muscles, golden skin—tiny flat caramel-colored nipples. Pierce wanted to taste it all, but Hal's mouth was too delicious to leave.

He kissed and allowed his hand to roam, playing with the tightened ends of the nipple candy and gliding his palm down the smooth skin of Hal's stomach.

And still that kiss went on, Pierce's replete body howling for intimate knowledge of the man who had so pleased him.

He slid his hand under Hal's waistband and groaned at the decadence of the hardened flesh under his palm.

"Jesus, Hal, you're huge," he breathed, squeezing the base and tightening his grip over the shaft.

Hal half sobbed into his mouth. "Ah... oh God... just... keep... oh please...."

Pierce pushed up to move so he could taste too, remember the feeling of a cock down his throat, luxuriate in the taste of another man's spend. Hal shook his head and captured Pierce with his hands, holding him there for more kisses, intimate and blistering, while Pierce grasped him hard and stroked.

The first spill of hot precome from the head was torture. Pierce *wanted* it, *craved* the feel of it spurting down the back of his throat. But Hal kept up with the kisses, so Pierce kept stroking until Hal cried out, "Slow! Hard! Squeeze the... ohmigod omigod omigod.... *Pierce!*"

Ah! Pierce bucked against Hal's hip, spilling a little bit himself as the first thick spurt oiled the rest of that amazing member. Pierce kept squeezing, touching, fondling, until the final spend, and Hal whimpered a little, sore.

Pierce pulled his hand up to his mouth, but Hal stopped him, eyes anxious and searching in the darkness.

"I need to get tested," he whispered, head turned like he was ashamed.

"Do," Pierce told him, wiping his hand off on the sheets and going in for a kiss. "I want to—"

Hal took his mouth hard, clinging, pulling back right when Pierce's entire brain was about to obliviate. "Why?" he asked while their harsh breathing returned to normal. "Why did you...?"

"I wanted it to be real," Pierce told him, his voice a faint rumble and not a whisper. "I wanted us to touch."

Hal closed his eyes, like that hurt, and swallowed. "I'll get tested tomorrow," he promised.

"Did you think I wouldn't understand?" Pierce's turn to lay his head on Hal's shoulder. "Did you think I'd judge you?"

"I wanted you to… to think I was a grown-up," Hal confessed, voice breaking a little. "All your talk about being old and cynical. I… wanted to be a grown-up and still a unicorn. So you'd know…."

"Shh…." Pierce's turn to silence the roaring in Hal's heart. He rolled a bit and kissed Hal, taking the sadness and the worry away. "Shh…." He kissed him again, just the slip of a tongue, not arousing but kind, healing. "You'll always be a unicorn," he promised. "You'll be forty-five and a unicorn. Or sixty. Just because I'm not as strong as you are doesn't mean I don't believe in you."

Hal shook his head and buried his face in the hollow of Pierce's shoulder. "You are," he hiccupped. "You are a unicorn. You just won't see…."

Pierce didn't know what to do with that. He nuzzled Hal's temple until his breathing quieted down some and Pierce could close his eyes and fall fast asleep.

FUTURE SHOCKS

"YOU CAN wait out in the car," Hal said, fidgeting with his key fob. "This'll take—"

"Anywhere from ten minutes to an hour," Pierce gauged, looking the medical clinic over grimly. "Anything hospital inclined is a crapshoot."

"I can drop you off at Walmart—it's right down the road." Hal still wouldn't look at him.

"Dammit!" Pierce snapped. "Hal! This isn't the end of the world! It's an HIV test—I got my first one in college." *Oh God—Ass. Hole.* Pierce took a deep breath and tried to be a unicorn, which was hard since Hal had been an evasive sprite all damned morning about the HIV test thing.

"I hate making you a part of my bad decision-making," Hal said after a moment, and oh holy crap and pass the potatoes, something *real*.

Pierce took a deep breath. "Forgetting the rubber happens." He let out a laugh. "Ask my sister. I wasn't joking when I said shaming people for sexual activity is high on my list of douchebag things to do."

"But it wasn't just once," Hal muttered, staring out the window. "I broke up with Russ, and Russ called me all sorts of… you know, prude and baby, and I was a stupid dumbass kid about it and set out to…." He flailed, avoiding Pierce's eyes like Pierce was a red-eyed dragon who hypnotized his prey.

"Set out to fuck everything that moved to prove him wrong?" Oh Lord, college.

Hal looked at him sideways—but at least he looked at him. "After Loren?" he said softly.

"After Katrina," Pierce said with a grimace. "First relationship. Freshman year. True love always, until Derrick found out she'd done everybody at school while we were going out."

"Ouch!"

Pierce shrugged—distance gave perspective. "You know, everybody has their damage. Whatever happened to *her* to make her need that? And I really do believe it was something she felt compelled to do—breaking up hurt her, mostly because she felt like she couldn't help herself. But yeah. I went out to prove I could bang all the things." Pierce did the unthinkable then—they'd had sexual activity and they'd even had kissing, but they hadn't yet done this.

He reached out and grabbed Hal's hand and brought the knuckles to his lips.

"I had a friend," he said, smiling a little before holding Hal's hand to his cheek. God, tenderness. He wanted to give Hal *all* the tenderness. "Derrick came to clubs with me and fucked all the things too. I forgot rubbers left and right and pretended I was hip and devil-may-care. Derrick forgot once and had a panic attack. So I… I said, 'Hey, let's just go check it out together, so we can not freak out about it,' right?"

"You were both negative, right?"

"Right," Pierce said, nodding. "I wouldn't bullshit you. But I had blood tests run in the hospital anyway—I would have told you that first night, Hal." He frowned. "Although I wish you'd asked."

Hal swallowed and tugged at his hand. Pierce let him go with some disappointment, but then Hal turned his palm and cupped Pierce's cheek.

"I'll get tested now," he said, stroking Pierce's lower lip with his thumb. "And… and I'll remember to ask the… if… uh, if I ever need to again."

Pierce kissed the inside of his palm and moved away so he could open the door and climb out with his cane. He avoided saying the obvious thing, the thing neither of them were saying.

They had less than a week and a half. Unless they decided to make this a long-distance thing, he was getting tested so they could share a handful of nights together.

The thought left a terrible ache, an empty void in the center of Pierce's chest.

Today. I'll be with him today. And tomorrow. And the next day. It will have to be good enough.

FIFTEEN MINUTES later they came out of the clinic, Hal looking disgustedly at his phone.

"They'll call me in one or two days?" he asked, upset.

"That's what they said," Pierce said mildly.

"Two days."

"So they said."

"We have to wait two days?"

"I hate to tell you this, but I can still give you blowjobs. You heard the guy—the risk of HIV through swallowing is—"

"Too big to risk," Hal snapped, glaring at him. "Handsies all the way."

Pierce glared at him, making diabolical, slow, and sensual plans that would make "handsies" look like a gift from the gods. "Sure," he said. "Handsies. 'Cause we're fourteen-year-olds grabbing each other in the locker room. Handsies."

Hal unlocked the doors with a gentle beep, hiding a smirk.

"What?" Pierce asked, swinging into the CR-V and cursing the stiffness left over from his morning workout. Dammit—he was seriously going to have to keep swimming if he ever wanted to move again.

If he ever wanted to possess Hal, completely, or pull his knees up to his chest and let Hal take him.

"Thirteen," Hal said, closing the door and starting the car. "I was thirteen, old man. What? Did you save your hand job cherry for college?"

"Graduation," Pierce muttered, embarrassed. "Some of us were *not* that cute in high school."

Hal paused in the act of pulling his seat belt on. "What makes you think some of us *were*? Cute in high school, I mean."

Pierce rolled his eyes. "Do I have to say it?" he asked, mortally embarrassed. "Are you really going to make me tell you this?"

Hal stared at him through those big amber eyes. Pierce had noticed, this last week, how lush his black eyelashes were, how strong his nose was, straight bridged and not too big. What a strong jaw he had, and how his smile was as innocent and bright as his mouth was sinfully wicked.

"Tell me what?"

Truth was a compulsion. "You're beautiful," Pierce said, embarrassed. "You... I was so embarrassed, that first day, because you were so pretty—so beautiful, and you were talking to me, and I was at my worst in my entire life. I couldn't even see your eyes then. And your eyes are beautiful. And your mouth is beautiful. I don't know how you could have been anything but beautiful in high school. I... I just don't understand."

It was his turn to look away, avoiding Hal's eyes.

Hal fumbled for his hand, but Pierce still couldn't have looked at him.

"I *so* would have blown you when I was in high school," Hal said fervently.

"And that would have made me a creepy old guy molesting an underage boy."

Hal laughed shortly. "Look at me. We're wasting gas."

Pierce turned reluctantly because he was right. "What?"

"I'm twenty-three."

"I know that."

"I'm only a little stupid."

Pierce couldn't help the faint smile. "Aren't we all."

"I wanted you from that first day. Hurt and pale—it didn't matter."

"Because you're crazy," Pierce said slowly, like you spoke to crazy people so as not to set them off.

Hal dragged the knuckles of his free hand down the side of Pierce's scarred cheek. "Because you're a unicorn," he said. Then he kissed Pierce, one of the softest, most tender kisses Pierce could ever remember. Aching with gentleness, it undid him, leveled everything in his heart, in his mind, that could have stood against Hal's incursion into his soul.

Hal pulled away and stroked his lower lip again. "Don't try to deny it," he whispered, and while Pierce was looking for words that wouldn't shatter either of them, Hal pulled away from the clinic. "So—should we try for wrapping paper this time?"

"How about rubbers and lube," Pierce muttered, unsettled and vulnerable. "We could start there."

"Sure. Zombie Apocalypse Central, here we come."

THEY REMEMBERED wrapping paper, ribbon, condoms, and lubricant.

They forgot scissors and tape.

"I don't even believe this," Hal said as he stared at the paper on the table in disbelief. "This is… this is *epic*. I'm, like, if I never see another Target for the rest of my life, it will be too soon for me in my next life and the guy I bang after that!"

"How can Derrick not have any scissors?" Pierce asked, rifling through the drawers. "I mean, we bought ribbon—if I just had, you know, scissors, I could cut the ribbon and wrap everything and use the ribbon to secure it."

Hal turned his head to gaze at Pierce in disbelief. "So you admit to being a Boy Scout, but you're going to deny the unicorn thing?"

Pierce wrinkled his nose. "Fine. Yes. Whatever." He flopped down in the love seat, which was where Hal usually sat when they watched television. "I'm at a loss," he said, shaking his head. "I say I skip Christmas at my sister's, turn down the job, and start living at the beach. You can throw me money when you visit from college."

"That's not a plan!" Hal told him, horror coloring his voice.

"It is too," Pierce insisted. "It's a plan. It's very much a plan."

"Well, it's a *shitty* plan. How about you stay here, watch some TV, and let me go get scissors and tape at the little drugstore up at the corner. They're crappy for Christmas shopping, but scissors and tape they can handle."

Pierce gazed at him in naked gratitude. "I would do unmentionable things to and for you just so I didn't have to go to Target again."

Hal rolled his eyes. "Same here." He handed Pierce the remote control and bent down, squeezing his shoulder and nuzzling his temple. "Nap. I'll get takeout. We'll work out double tomorrow, how's that?"

Perfect.

PIERCE JERKED awake about an hour later, looking around the condo muzzily. He'd fallen asleep watching a rerun of *2 Broke Girls* and now a rerun of *Castle* had taken its place. Hal had opened the shades over the sliding glass doors, and the sun, which had been sulking behind clouds and haze when he'd first sat down, was now glaring at him on the horizon.

He yawned and stretched, trying to remember if he'd heard Hal return.

Takeout boxes sat on the table—unopened and still steaming—so he must have been there somewhere.

Pierce stood, shivering, and made his way over the rubber mats toward the bedroom, wondering if Hal had gone down for a nap of his own. He approached the doorway, which stood dark, and heard Hal's voice.

"No, I haven't decided. I told you that ten minutes ago." He paused, and in the darkness, Pierce could see him stretched horizontally on the bed, facing the window and not the doorway. "You said I had until after New Year's—why is this a problem?" He grunted and swung his feet over his bottom, the gesture absurdly young. "What do I *want* you to do? Well, maybe not kick me out for Christmas—that would be a start. But how about letting me get my massage therapy certificate—I mean, I could go for sports medicine if you want, but I've been trying to get that done between my coursework for two years. You have to know I mean it by now!"

Whatever the reply, it was *not* what he wanted to hear. He groaned and rolled over to his back. "Yeah! I get it! I'm not good enough to be your kid anyway—you've made that clear!" He spotted Pierce and held out his hand.

For a moment, Pierce thought about retreating into the living room to give him his "space," but two things stopped him.

One was that Hal had been there—two of the worst phone calls of his life, and Hal had been there, holding, supporting—making love. Pierce couldn't just leave him to work out his own shit.

But Pierce didn't *want* to leave him—that was the second thing.

He stepped into the room and threw himself lengthwise on the bed next to Hal, then rolled over on his side and slid his hand up under Hal's T-shirt so he was touching bare skin.

Hal captured his hand and clung.

"No, I'm not being overdramatic—and it's not a gay thing. You don't want me home because I'm gay—excuse the hell out of me for being gay. You don't want me to leech off your fortune unless I'm doing something worthwhile. Like be a lawyer. And only be a lawyer. And be nothing else but a lawyer."

The next thing over the phone made him sit up explosively, and Pierce had to scramble to sit next to him.

"How do I know that? Because I've been telling you. Yes I have. Yes I have. No, yes I have! I've been *telling you for years* that I want to do something else. Well, maybe if you'd have let me take the general ed I wanted to instead of the prelaw, I would have had a better idea sooner, but I know now!" He took a deep breath through the next flurry of conversation—from a woman, it sounded like, so Mom, probably—and then blurted, "If you guys cared at all about who I *am* instead of who you *want me to be*, maybe this wouldn't sound like drama to you!"

He listened for another minute and then burst out, "I'll tell you after New Year's like I said I would! No! *Don't* call me on Christmas Day, because I don't give a fuck what you're doing, just like you don't give a *fuck* about me!"

He hit End Call, but that apparently wasn't satisfying enough, because he cocked his arm back, and Pierce had to rescue the phone.

"Oh oh oh! Hold up there, Chief—if you're thinking about going solo without backup, paying for a phone is a bad way to start."

Hal let go of the phone and threw himself back onto the bed, scrubbing his face with his hands. "Augh!"

Pierce lay down next to him again, keeping that bare skin contact with his hand to the soft skin of Hal's taut middle.

"I'm so pissed!" Hal raged. "Called me up right when I pulled in, and it was all, 'Why haven't you signed up for classes?' and I was all 'Because you gave me extra time!' and they were all...." He took a deep breath and shook his head. "Like it was all predetermined. That I would go be this thing they wanted me to be and I wouldn't argue with them, and it would all be okay."

"They *really* don't know you very well," Pierce said, pulling air from the hollow of his neck and shoulder.

Hal turned so quickly their lips touched before he had a chance to decide. Pierce went with it, parting his lips, delving into his sweet mouth for a few breaths, a few heartbeats. Hal pulled back, and he almost keened.

God, he wanted all the time he could possibly get.

"Why do you say that?" Hal asked softly.

"They don't know you?" Pierce frowned. "Because... you're not... docile. You... you push back. You fight. You make decisions. I... I know you're young." He grimaced. "But God, Hal, do you think we'd be... do you think I'd... I mean, I wouldn't be having a relationship with you if you didn't know who you are."

A slow smile spread over Hal's godsbedamned beautiful face. "I was a pushover with Russ," he rasped. "I've been a good kid all my life. When push came to shove, I think they just expected me to...."

"Bend over and take it?" Pierce said throatily. There was no question at all—none—who would top between them. Who would have his hands most comfortably on the reins, who would gauge the situation, the heat of their bodies, the susceptibility of flesh, more competently of the two of them.

Pierce could top, was comfortable doing so—but Hal was *made* to be in control.

Hal blinked, slowly, expression turning sultry in the dim light of late afternoon. "I will *take* you," he promised. "I will... I will shove myself so far inside you that you'll taste me coming when I'm in your ass."

Pierce closed his eyes, hard, painfully hard, at the sound of Hal's voice promising dire things. "That will happen," he promised rashly, because what if he couldn't? His body was looser now, but still—not

100 percent. Creeping past 50 percent. He leaned close to Hal's ear and whispered, "I want you inside me so bad…."

Hal's sound—raw, wanting, primal—did things to Pierce's body that actual sex had missed. Oh man—how could he have lived this long and not known what it was like to be wanted like that?

With a feral growl, Hal rolled over, lying on top of Pierce and claiming his mouth in a hard, wet mauling of a kiss. His tongue swept inside, and Pierce's defenses disintegrated, his good sense annihilated at the hard pressure of Hal's groin against his.

Pierce yanked at his shirt, wanting that chest—golden, soft skinned, hard muscled—under his hands. He was *starving* for touch like this, for Hal's mouth slanting over his again and again and again.

Hal moved faster than he did, and he pulled back to haul his shirt over his head and shove his jeans and underwear down off his feet, finishing before Pierce could even unbutton his own shirt.

Hal took over the task with shaking fingers.

"You"—button—"are trying"—button—"to kill me." Button, button, button.

Pierce opened his arms so Hal could help him struggle out of the shirt, and then his T-shirt.

"I need you alive," Pierce told him as Hal yanked at the waistband of his cargo shorts. Pierce lifted up his ass and let them be hauled down.

They paused for a moment, naked in the twilight, vulnerable and wanting.

Hal groaned and crashed his mouth down again, his hand going straight for Pierce's cock.

Well, two could play at that game.

It was a rough, rocky race to the finish line, a carnal stroking of each other's cocks while their mouths never stopped the mutual ravishing. Hal's hand was a rough, strong wonder on Pierce's erection—no finesse, no titillation. Pure hand-fucking that made the phrase "handsies" even more juvenile—a diminishment of the power knotting Pierce's belly, his thighs, his taint.

He groaned into Hal's mouth, brought abruptly to the edge of a spinning climax, and Hal bucked and spurted, apparently hitting his own peak just that fast.

"Ah!" Pierce broke off from the kiss, wanting to revel in the feeling of come over his fingers. Hal bit his neck, hard enough to leave a mark, and again, lower, and again, sucking the flesh in his mouth without apology.

Pierce gave Hal's cock one more frantic, expert stroke, squeezing at the head, oiling the whole member with the precome. Hal bit his shoulder and growled, bucking, coming undone in Pierce's hand while Pierce let the white light and tumbling surf of climax crash over them both.

When their bodies had stopped convulsing, they were left in a trembling, chilly aftermath, breathing harshly into the shadows of each other's flesh.

"Eventually," Hal panted, "we're going to need condoms."

"Sure," Pierce said. He thought, *Once you're inside me, I don't know if I can ever leave you.*

Oh hells. Oh God, oh hells, oh damn.

Hal, a week and a half isn't going to be enough.

THE NEXT morning, Hal really did double down on the workout to make up for their laziness the night before. Pierce went along with it—well, he grumbled about slave drivers and torturers and fucking sadists until the older couple who had been thinking about coming to the pool toward the end of the workout looked at each other in alarm and retreated—but by God, he did it.

He still had the idea that maybe he'd be up to using the condoms and the lubricant by the time he left for Sasha's.

Artificial deadline, you fuckwad.

Yeah, his inner voice was bitter, but it was hard to talk it off the ledge when he was pushing so hard he could barely breathe.

"Okay, slow that down a little," Hal said. "We're doing the open-gaited run—not so fast, but active stretching. Make sure you stretch a *lot*, because—" He paused in his torture and grinned lasciviously. "—well, just because."

Pierce wanted to roll his eyes, but he also wanted to do more of what they'd been doing at night, so he refrained.

The overbright *ting* of Hal's phone cutting through the music it played made them both pause. "Don't stop!" Hal snapped, and Pierce *did* manage not to roll his eyes—but he didn't stop.

"Hello. Hal Lombard." Suddenly Hal went very still. Pierce paused to look at him in concern, and Hal didn't stop him. "Yes? Yes. Negative?"

The slow smile across his face told Pierce the negative was exactly what they'd been hoping for. He caught Hal's eyes and smiled.

"Thank you. Yes—happy holidays to you too."

He hit End Call and the music resumed, but Pierce didn't head toward the other side of the pool. "Negative?" he asked softly.

Hal bit his lip and nodded. "Yeah."

"Good."

Hal frowned. "*You* need to get moving again or you're going to cramp like a guy kidnapped in the trunk of a car. Now go!"

"Sadist."

"Whatever. Do you want a rubdown in the hot tub?"

Yes. I want a rubdown in the hot tub, and in the bed, and all over my body.

"Maybe."

"Then move your ass, Pierce—thataboy!"

Pierce finished his workout with a minimum of fuss. He'd seen the soft smile, the pleased relief. He'd been a part of that.

He'd be a part of the celebration too.

THAT NIGHT Pierce wrapped presents while Hal finished the Lego Christmas tree.

"Do you want me to wrap your bear?" Pierce asked, just to make sure.

"It's the only thing I'm going to have to open," Hal told him without self-pity. "Of course."

"Okay, then. Just remember the Legos are yours too."

Hal grinned at him with the glee of a five-year-old. "Yeah?"

"Of course they are!" Pierce grinned back. He would have to give Hal Legos for Christmas every year.

Shit. Crap. Whatever.

Pierce would get his address and send him Legos for Christmas every year, even if that was the only time ever after they talked to each other after Pierce left on the twenty-fourth.

That was a promise he made himself. Legos for Hal Lombard, forever. It was a deal.

Hal was concentrating on putting details on the tree, though. Teeny-tiny corner pieces in red, blue, and yellow served as Christmas tree lights. Pierce was very impressed.

Pierce, clumsy this year but still able, wrapped the Keurig and the two giant teddy bears and the big boxes with glee. He wanted to give Hal something else, he thought as he arranged the gifts on the floor near the end table, where the Christmas tree would go.

"What do massage therapists *need*?" he asked himself.

Hal didn't even look up. "We need a certificate," he said promptly. "From a reputable school or apprentice program, and about 500 hours of practice. In some states it's 1100. Who knows."

Pierce grimaced cheerfully—you couldn't say his boy wasn't focused. "I mean materially. Is there a kind of massage oil you like? Do you need a folding table? What *things* do you need to be a massage therapist?"

Hal shrugged. "A sturdy table—the kind that can hold up to 500 pounds but wheels in on its own. Massage oil. An internship. It's pretty simple, but it takes dedication. And, you know, not being a dick with people's bodies. I mean, I took a couple summer classes and have about 300 hours, but it's not close yet."

"Okay," Pierce said, thinking hard. "Okay."

"So, what do you think? Should I add non-Lego touches? Ribbon? Cotton balls? Tinsel?"

Pierce looked at it critically. "I think non-Lego touches would be awesome. Come on, raid the stash pile—let's see what you can do."

"Yeah, well, thank God for tape. Okay—here we go."

Pierce finished stacking his gifts and sat down at the laptop desk while Hal worked away, industrious and absorbed. Some of the fury of their lovemaking the night before had abated, but the underlying tension, that continual need, was gnawing away at Pierce's stomach.

He was going to *need* Hal again that night. He was going to *need* him in the morning. Pierce had been mildly paranoid about becoming addicted to pain pills when he'd been released from the hospital— he'd had no idea his most frightening addiction would be the body of the pushy aqua instructor who had just sort of bossed his way into Pierce's life.

How did you recover from that?

He started searching the internet for massage tables, not even batting an eyelash at the prices. He could do it. He *should* do it. He should buy Hal a massage table, so when he decided not to take his parents' prefab life, he could have a head start into the life of his own.

Two things stopped him from just pushing the button.

The first was that delivery wouldn't be until after he left for Sasha's. He imagined Hal, sad and alone—and possibly hungover— the day after Christmas, getting the massage table from the lover who'd wandered into his life and then wandered out again.

He imagined him trying to set a world record for bingeing on greyhounds. He imagined the headline "College Student Dies of Alcohol Poisoning After Receiving a Really Expensive Gift from a Thoughtless Bastard."

Imagined smashing his own head against his keyboard until the computer didn't go anymore.

But that was only the first thing.

The second thing was that, even if Hal got it and loved it—took it and became a world-class massage therapist who catered to the stars and owed it all to Pierce and his fabulous gift and the faith he had such a short time to impart—it wouldn't be enough.

It would feel like a real expensive tip to a therapist—and that's not what Pierce wanted to give him at all.

"Ta-da!"

Pierce had no idea how long he was lost in an agony of indecision, but he turned around, and Hal stood holding the Lego Christmas tree out in front of him with all the aplomb of an excited twelve-year-old.

Pierce's heart almost throbbed right out of his chest.

"Let me get a picture," he said, his smile hurting his cheeks. "C'mon, stand right there—" He motioned to the light, and Hal moved to the optimum spot, a proud smile on his face.

Pierce took the picture, and then another one, and then three more, before Hal snatched the camera out of his hand.

"Jesus, nobody needs that many pictures of me!"

"I do," Pierce defended grumpily. "It's important."

"Whatever. Here—selfie with the tree!"

"That's not gonna—"

"Ugh."

They both stared at the picture, with Pierce's eyes half open and a Lego Christmas tree sprouting from Hal's mouth like a deformed tooth.

"Okay—just us." Hal set the tree down and looped his arm over Pierce's shoulder, and both of them smiled at the phone with such optimism and hope, Pierce almost didn't believe it was him in that picture. Hal snapped it, then grabbed the phone.

"Here," he said, and his voice dropped like he'd realized, hey, this might be the only evidence that both of them ever existed in the same space and made multiple trips to Target and dominated the pool in the morning and sometimes took halting, pointless, beautiful walks along the beach. "Let me send it to my phone."

"So I have your contacts," Pierce said, which sounded obvious, but they hadn't done that yet. Exchanging numbers would mean they were thinking about beyond this moment.

Hal looked up at him sideways. "So I can look at your smile," he said.

Pierce nodded, his throat tight. "I can text you the next time I go to Target."

Hal's laughter sounded false to his ears, but Pierce didn't have the heart to look him in the eyes. "Here," he said quietly. "Set it on the end table—I'll text Sasha. She can show the kids."

The neighbor made a Christmas tree—we're both very proud.

He sent one of the ones with Hal and one with the wrapped presents, both looking festive and out of place in the bright bold and white of the condo, and then sent the same thing to Derrick.

Neither responded, but as Pierce looked up, he realized something.

"Hey," he said, musing. "Don't you have a bestie? A buddy? A girl you wish you could marry? Something?"

Hal shrugged, ambling away from the Christmas corner, looking embarrassed. "I, uh, lost my peer group in the divorce," he said, trying to look like it was no big deal. "And... well, I took a lot of different classes. No time to hang out with the other biology majors or history majors because... you know...."

"You were taking six other things," Pierce said, getting it— but only a little. The answer hit him then, and his stomach knotted. "Tough being a judge's son?"

Hal screwed his eyes shut and flopped on the small couch. "You have no idea."

"All the kids in high school were—"

"Affluent, white, and shitty to other people," Hal muttered. "Yeah. I mean, the gay thing, fine. The massage-therapist thing?"

"Not so fine," Pierce said, getting it. "I went to a commuter school. If you weren't in the same major, you just didn't meet that many people."

Hal cocked his head. "Why a commuter school?"

Pierce shrugged. "Not much money, I guess." He thought about it, suddenly feeling like a crappy human being. "I had to help Sasha through school, but I guess I wouldn't have gotten through without my parents."

Hal looked like he wanted to say something—desperately. But he bit his lip and grabbed the remote instead.

"Wabbit season," he said softly.

"Duck season." Suddenly all Pierce wanted to do was kill time until they could be bodies moving in the dark.

THAT NIGHT, as they stood up to go to bed, he moved quickly enough to wrap his arms around Hal's waist and whisper in his ear.

"Go in, get undressed, lie naked on the bed." At Hal's indrawn breath, he added, "Turn off the light and close your eyes."

He heard Hal's swallow and let him go ahead while Pierce got the lights and locked up. On his way, he grabbed the lubricant off the table, where it had sat, chaste, in its little bag with the condoms.

He left the condoms on the table—his body was sore from the extra workout that morning, and cramping up in the middle of sex was not attractive.

Besides. He wanted to take care of Hal tonight.

When he got to the room, he paused to let his eyes adjust to the dark. And because he wanted to see Hal, legs splayed indecently, naked and vulnerable.

And for that night, his.

He undressed as quickly as he could, leaving his boxers up near his pillow to make them easier to find when they were done, and then, without saying a word, positioned himself between Hal's knees.

He heard the little gasp that meant Hal felt him, and then ran his hands up and down Hal's calves. Hal groaned softly, so Pierce followed through on the caress, behind the knees to his inner thighs. Pierce didn't know anything about massage, but he did know about the wonders of skin against skin.

He ran both hands to Hal's inner thighs, where he could run palms around the soft flesh of his legs and his thumbs down the juncture of leg and erogenous zone. When he extended the caress to part Hal's asscheeks, Hal's groan almost rocked him off the bed.

Pierce stretched out on his stomach, putting most of his weight on his good side, and bent his head, tracing a path with his tongue where his thumbs had been.

"Killing. Me."

Hal's voice, loud and demanding in the dark, startled Pierce badly enough to slip, face-planting with his mouth over Hal's balls.

Disgruntled, he sucked one into his mouth, pleased when Hal's feet came off the bed and he made a happy, turned-on sound.

"Okay, okay, okay," Hal whispered. "No talking."

Pierce sucked a little harder in acknowledgment and positioned himself again, this time with his hand on Hal's thickening cock.

He licked a line between his fingers and his thumb—because there was a space between them, because damn. He got to the bell and played, excited because tonight was his turn. He widened his mouth and lowered his head, letting his lips barely brush the head, his tongue flutter around it, while his hot breath promised the cave of wonders was *right there*.

Hal grunted and tried to buck but held himself back.

Pierce repaid him with a lick over the head, while his other hand fumbled for the lube bottle. Hal groaned, and Pierce gave another butterfly lick, and another, tasting precome.

"You know what that means," Pierce whispered into the darkness. "You want to swallow?"

Just hearing the words was dirty enough to make Pierce hard.

"Sure." He tightened his mouth then and lowered his head, putting pressure all the way down to the root. Hal moaned and massaged Pierce's scalp through his hair while Pierce wiggled on the bed and tried to remember his plan.

Oh yes.

Lubricant.

He one-handed the bottle while he worked, his weaker arm trembling for the seconds it took to make his fingers slick and snap the top back on.

But once that was done, he could explore, sliding his fingertips down the center of Hal's warm cleft, finding the pucker in the center. A part of him yearned for sunlight and an entire day to make love, but most of him knew that his body had maybe a half an hour in it.

He would make it count.

He slid a fingertip inside and played the edge of Hal's bell with his tongue and the very delicate edge of his teeth. Hal let out a deep shudder and hunched down on the finger, taking Pierce up to his second knuckle.

"Getting cheeky," Pierce whispered, making sure his breath ghosted over the wet skin of Hal's cockhead.

"Not. A. Virgin," Hal graveled from a constricted throat.

Pierce grunted and took Hal's cock all the way down to the back of his throat—and added another finger.

The sound Hal let out was not quite human.

Oh, he was tight. His ass clamped down hard on Pierce's fingers, and Pierce thrust them in deeper and then pulled them out. Hal planted his feet farther apart and lifted his hips, giving Pierce free rein, and

Pierce took it, lowering his mouth to the root and shoving his fingers in harder.

Hal moaned, shaking, and spurted just a little bit of pre.

But he didn't come. Not yet.

Pierce added a little more lube—and then he added, very slowly, another finger.

Hal screamed into his forearm, and Pierce thrust hard, digging his tongue into the slit at the top and widening his fingers at the root on the bottom.

Pierce knew himself, knew he'd be gibbering by now, begging, *needing*, but Hal—Hal kept more inside. He grabbed his thighs, spreading himself wider, and Pierce fucked him harder, sucking him, swirling his tongue for all he was worth.

Hal let out a groan and let go of his thighs. He banged his hands into the bed as he chased his elusive orgasm, and Pierce changed tactics.

He kept his fingers in the searing heat of Hal's body but started to move them *slowly*. He pulled his head back to torment the head of Hal's cock, but he used his other hand to squeeze and stroke *slowly*.

He continued to tease—tongue and the faintest edge of his teeth—but he went *slowly*.

Hal lost his mind.

His arms went first, flailing and pounding the bed on either side, and Pierce stopped for a moment, fingers still fucking, and issued an order. "Your nipples, Hal—pinch them!"

Hal did what he suggested, and Pierce kept up the slow pressure, the caress, the driving Hal out of his mind.

He kept squeezing the head of Hal's cock whenever he got to the end of the stroke and... one more time... and another... and another... and....

Hal screamed, his chest lifting off the bed like he was being hauled up by strings, his head tilted back as he cried out. Pierce didn't stop, not even when his mouth flooded, and he had to swallow, and again.

Hal collapsed against the bed in a limp heap, whimpering, "Done. I'm done," and Pierce finally stopped. He wiped his fingers on a washcloth he'd brought, and wiped his mouth on his bare shoulder while Hal curled up on his side self-protectively and caught his breath.

"Pierce?" he said, voice quavery in the moonlight coming from the window.

"Yeah?"

"Come here. I need to kiss you."

Pierce didn't ask if he'd mind tasting his own come—that was part of the celebration, he figured. He scooted up to lay his head on the pillow, and Hal took his mouth, sweeping his tongue in, taking over again and again and again. Pierce kissed him back, aroused, but just as happy to neck in the dark until they fell asleep.

But Hal had words for him before that happened.

"That was amazing," he whispered, and Pierce smiled, justifiably proud.

"You're fun to make love to," he said. He couldn't remember another lover—not Cynthia, not Loren—who would have abandoned himself so thoroughly. "I could suck your cock for a month."

Hal laughed weakly, but he was apparently thinking about something else. "I'm... I think tomorrow I'm going to go get you a gift. Is that okay?"

Pierce smiled, though, darkness and all. "Okay but not necessary," he said, nuzzling Hal's sweaty chest.

"I... I need to do something else, though, up in my condo." Hal grunted. "Just, you know, some housecleaning stuff. I haven't really been living there. I should...."

Pierce frowned. "You don't want to move ba—"

"No! Not... not until I have to." Hal let out a frustrated puff of air. "Just... tonight, I took care of my old business, and you did something really awesome for me. And I just want to take care of my old business again. But I don't want you to have to—"

Pierce shoved up on his good elbow. "You've done nothing this month but deal with me and my old business," he accused. "Why wouldn't I want to help you with—?"

Hal kissed him, hard, demandingly, until Pierce was an amoeba, melting into the mattress. "Please," he whispered. "I don't want you to see me like... like the condo would let you see me."

Pierce scowled, but he had to admit—he'd been out-bossed. "I could take it," he protested, feeling young and protected and not liking it. "I actually *am* older than you."

Hal laughed and kissed his cheek. "Believe me, Captain Recovery, I am aware. Just…." He licked the corner of his own mouth delicately, where a shiny drop of come threatened to trickle down. "You let me be the boss between us," he said after a moment, running his hand over Pierce's naked chest.

"Maybe I'm just naturally submissive," Pierce admitted, feeling like that was a big step.

Hal's raucous laughter told him maybe he hadn't said anything that insightful after all. "You think?" He ran his hand to Pierce's groin and began to tickle. "It's why we need you stretched and mobile, my friend—you have the makings of a sexual dynamo, and we just need recovery to free it. Like letting the Tasmanian devil out of his cage."

Pierce chuckled weakly and allowed Hal to fondle his cock.

"Feels like you came already," Hal said, nuzzling Pierce's bicep.

"I did, a little." Pierce smiled complacently, so happy in this moment he was surprised he had the wherewithal to speak. "I… this here? Us. You in my mouth? It's perfect."

Hal dropped his head to rest it on Pierce's shoulder. "Yeah."

They didn't mention the deadline or the things they might not get a chance to do.

It was the only time in Pierce's life that he was content to let "perfect" just exist, even if it might not be "permanent."

'TWAS THE NIGHT BEFORE

TRUE TO his word, Hal disappeared for a few hours the next day, right after their time at the pool. Pierce used the time to talk with his new employers and to take a look at the projects he'd be starting in March. He readily admitted to himself that the job would be a lot more fun than his old one—he seemed to have landed on his feet there, and another layer of the depression that had dogged him when he'd arrived at the condo peeled away.

I'm a provider again. I can even provide for… a college student. Or a massage therapy student. Or a dog. Or whatever.

Oh, the things he didn't want to think about.

He spent two hours writing a research-and-development plan for something he wasn't supposed to do for two months, just to avoid the thing he might have to do in slightly more than a week.

Hal showed up in the late afternoon, teeth chattering and lips almost blue with cold.

Pierce greeted him, holding his fingers and rubbing. "What in the hell?"

"Power's off at the condo," Hal muttered. "Wish I'd known— had to throw out all the frozen food."

Pierce frowned. "Wait. Power's off? It's not off here?"

Hal turned away, jaw locked grimly. "My parents had it turned off in their unit. Told the manager it wasn't supposed to be occupied."

Pierce gaped. "Uh…."

Hal shrugged. "Yes, they knew this was where I was. Yes, it was a tactic to get me to cave. But when I told the manager I was here, he recognized me, assumed it was a mistake, and told me he'd have it back on tomorrow."

Pierce shivered and wrapped his arm around Hal's shoulders, wanting to warm him up from the inside out. "Did you get all your shopping done?" he asked hopefully.

"They canceled my credit cards," Hal muttered glumly. "But I've got a bank account they can't touch. I'll go into town tomorrow and get cash."

Oh hells. "Oh baby," Pierce murmured, holding him tighter. "I'm so sorry."

Hal shook his head—but sank into Pierce's hold. "I'm not," he said fiercely. "If they wanted to show me who they were, they couldn't have picked a better way to do it."

"But… but… what will you do… you know. After?" *After I leave. After I ride off into the sunset to be with my family when you've just realized you don't have family to speak of.*

"I have power until New Year's. I've got money. I've got a car. Don't worry, Pierce, I won't be homeless." Hal pulled away, not looking at him, and started hunting around the kitchen. "Did you cook?"

"We bought a roast—I threw in some onion soup and some carrots and some stewed tomatoes. It wasn't much."

"You cooked!"

Pierce had to smile, although he wasn't sure he could breathe. "Sure. We'll call it cooking."

Hal turned to him, face alight. "For me? You cooked *for me*?"

Come home with me. I'll cook for you forever.

Pierce almost said it out loud, which was ludicrous because he only had four or five things, tops, that he could make without embarrassment. One of them was ham. "Yeah," he choked. "Of course. You'd tell me, right?"

"Tell you what?"

Hal poked the contents of the slow cooker with the wooden spoon next to it and breathed in rapturously. "The meat's falling apart. Can I eat? It looks great. Let's eat!"

"If you were going to end up homeless. If you had nowhere to go. You'd tell me. You'd say, 'Hey, can I have some help here, 'cause we're friends and lovers and I know you don't want me to be alone and homeless and alone.'"

Hal looked over his shoulder. "You'd tell *me*, right? If you were going back to Sacramento to be alone and not homeless but still alone."

"It's not the same thing," Pierce rasped. He could see himself clearly, in his little house with the big yard, with no Cynthia, working until the wee hours of the night, until his body knotted up and he could barely move, all to avoid the sound of his house when there was nobody there.

Hal left the roast alone to kiss his cheek. "Sure it is," he said softly. "But I've got more than enough to rent an apartment and live on my own, so don't worry about it. Let's eat."

Wabbit season.

Duck season.

Lonely season.

Fuck season.

Wanting season.

Suck it season.

Crying season.

Denying season.

Pierce was beginning to see why that bit always ended in "Bang!"

HAL'S WHIMPERS woke him up at 4:00 a.m....

"Wha—?"

"Sorry." Even in the dark, Pierce could hear his teeth chattering. "Bad dream."

Pierce rolled over and pulled him close. He'd put on boxers after lovemaking that night, but Hal was still bare and naked, vulnerable under their little blanket fort. Pierce wrapped his arms around his shoulders and tried to be his human shield.

"Shh. It's okay, baby. Don't worry. Nobody's going to hurt you."

Except you, Pierce, you cowardly coward who cowers.

Hal didn't say it—maybe he didn't even think it. But it was there, drifting between Pierce's ears, even as Hal settled down and fell asleep.

THE WEEK passed so quickly. Aqua, rubdowns, walks that grew longer and longer. Pierce had always assumed that a vacation with nothing to do would be a death sentence of boredom—but not with

Hal. Sitting in front of the television was a treat. Surfing the net or working was a treat.

Just hearing him breathe in the same room was a treat.

And after his mysterious trips to clean out the condo—and how much damage could he have done in two days? Pierce was starting to be seriously concerned—greeting Hal as he walked in the doorway was like Christmas and his birthday rolled into one.

Except on Christmas, Pierce would be gone, and Hal would be here, in his condo. With parents who could turn the heat off at any moment.

December 22, Pierce got a text from Sasha:

You're coming, right? Have you booked a car?

Pierce looked at the text and grimaced. Yes, he should probably try to book a car ahead of time.

Not yet.

Why not!

Busy.

With your friend?

Pierce sighed.

I don't want to leave him.

Invite him to come.

It's complicated.

Coming over for Christmas? So easy. I'm making ham. Feeds everybody.

Oh Jesus. Pierce's sister. Best. Human being. Ever.

If I invite him for Christmas, I'll invite him forever.

There was a pause, and Pierce wondered if he'd even mentioned he was sleeping with the neighbor.

THAT kind of friend?

Yes.

Good enough for forever?

Yes.

He stared at the word. Felt compelled to add:

He's young. He's just starting out. He's getting his massage certificate. What would he do with me, Sasha? I'm grumpy and divorced.

And still that incriminating silence.

And his whole life is here. And mine is in Sacramento.

He stared at the phone and willed his sister to text something.

And it's been a shitty year. Why would he follow me 3000 miles when there's other people here? I probably still can't drive. I don't want him to pity me.

And... nothing.

What if he said no?

He'd be almost as stupid as you are.

Sasha!

I'll book the car for twelve. If you cancel it for whatever reason, let me know.

He's TWENTY-THREE.

I love you, Pierce, but Jesus, you worry too much.

He was in the middle of typing "I love you too," when she texted again.

I don't feel like arguing either. If you show up here heartbroken I'll need my strength. TTYL

And that was that.

PIERCE WOKE up the morning of the twenty-third feeling the sort of despair in his stomach he hadn't felt since the hospital, except reversed.

In the hospital it had been *Oh shit, I'm in the hospital, and I'm trapped here until they say I can go home, and then I'm with Cynthia and I'm trapped there, and then I'm home, and that's worse.*

Now, the day before Christmas Eve, it was *Oh shit. I'm going to have a wonderful day with someone I love, and then I'm going to have to leave forever because....*

Why again?

Because grown men who knew how the world worked didn't fall in love in a month? In a week? In a day?

In the first hour, when I was pissed and he was hungover, and he helped me first and came on to me second?

"Hey," Hal said at his side.

Pierce rolled over to smile at him, holding the sheet up in front of his mouth because he'd caught himself snoring once or twice the night before and his breath could give dragons a run for their money.

"Hey," he said back. "Happy Christmas Adam."

Hal grinned and pulled the sheet away. "The day before Eve," he murmured, then touched lips with him.

Pierce gave up on protecting Hal and opened his mouth, all the things he wanted to say shorting out like a neon sign in a windstorm.

The kiss went long and deep, and Pierce moaned, needing.

Hal pulled away and smiled shyly. "So, you need to take a hot shower—"

"No workout?"

He shook his head. "No. No workout. Today is better than a workout. I'm going to get my massage table from upstairs—"

"You have a massage table?" Well, it was a good thing Pierce had chickened out, wasn't it!

"Yeah. I thought you knew that—you asked me what I needed. Anyway. I'm going to bring it down here and heat up the oils." He grinned as he swung out of bed. "That's going to be my Christmas present to you," he said, proud of himself. "A full-body massage, and then we'll make Christmas cookies—"

Pierce frowned. "You bought ingredients?" Hal had gone shopping the day before, while Pierce had been answering some questions with the new bosses online.

"I did." Hal grinned smugly. "And I bought a ham and some asparagus too, so we'll make cookies and then cook Christmas dinner and then…."

He grinned at Pierce with a predatory quirk to his eyebrows.

"What?" Pierce asked, actually breathless.

"We'll see how far you can stretch," Hal hummed. He twisted in the bed, leaned forward, and placed his lips right up against Pierce's ear. "I want inside you so bad."

Pierce's eyes honest to God rolled back in his head, and his chest tightened with the need to breathe.

"You want it too," Hal said, those amber eyes lit up from inside with lust and hellfire and unholy desire.

"So bad," Pierce moaned breathily.

"Merry Christmas to us."

Pierce nodded, completely helpless, his heart full of words that meant forever, his brain full of that light from Hal's smile.

THE MASSAGE table didn't seem like much—it came in folded, on wheels, with a little latch to hold it closed. Pierce got out of the shower and watched as Hal set up the table and put one sheet down on the bottom.

"I'm supposed to do this with two sheets," Hal said, sounding very professional. "Because not everybody wants to be all naked and stuff in front of someone who's just going to rub their muscles." He glanced up at Pierce and winked. "But I've seen all you got, so we only have to use it if you get cold. The one on the bottom is to sop up the extra oil so you don't slide around the table like a pancake on a griddle."

Heat rose up from the balls of Pierce's feet to flush across his neck. "I, uh, take it I'm the only one who gets the optional top sheet."

Hal laughed. "Yeah. I mean, people make a big deal about massage therapists and happy endings, but the fact is, getting a full-body massage is really a whole big… thing. A lot of people practically go into subspace when they're getting a body rub—muscles in their necks and back that haven't released in years suddenly don't hurt anymore. It's pretty euphoric."

"No sex necessary," Pierce said—he'd known this before, although he'd never gotten a massage himself.

"Oh, it's necessary," Hal purred, waggling his eyebrows. "But that's just because I want you. Really fucking bad."

"Again," Pierce said softly.

"It's not getting any less urgent," Hal agreed calmly. He swallowed and bit his lip shyly. "It's just this… this massage thing. It's different. It's not sex. I… it's something I do really well, and I wanted to… to *give* it to you."

Pierce got it. "It's my Christmas present," he repeated, delighted.

Hal nodded. "Exactly! I couldn't…." And now his bit lip seemed vulnerable. "I couldn't find anything good," he said finally. "Everything I found was an 'us' thing. I needed a 'you' thing. This thing—I mean, there's sex tonight, but it's ten in the morning. This thing is all about you."

Pierce studied his bare and bony feet for a moment. "Jesus, Harold. I just got you a teddy bear."

"And Legos," Hal said softly. "And you."

Pierce opened his mouth—not sure of what he'd say next—but Hal called him over. "If I was with a client, I'd leave the room, because, you know, privacy and professional. But here—give me the towel, I'll put it down where your crotch is supposed to go. Now lie flat, facedown—yeah, face in the face cradle when you get settled."

Pierce complied, taking his time because Hal was right. They *did* know each other—he *wasn't* self-conscious about how long it took to get situated, to place his limbs so they wouldn't hurt, to be in a position where touching would be okay.

"Now I'm going to put some music in—I'm going to use movie soundtracks, because most of the time those don't drive people bugshit, okay?"

Pierce had to smile. "Okay." He put his face in the face thing, and Hal adjusted it so it didn't feel like his neck was going to drop off, and then….

Transported was the only word.

Hal was right—it wasn't sexual, even though Pierce and Hal were sexual creatures to each other.

But it was *amazing*. Hal's cheerful, kind patter and his hard, no-bullshit hands just sort of… pushed all of the tension, all of the pain out of Pierce's body. They talked, like they always did. Telling stories, bullshitting, zinging one-liners, but the whole time Hal's hands, his careful, caring, marvelous hands were ridding Pierce of every angry toxin that had knotted his muscles from his toes to his tingling scalp. Toward the end, the conversation died, and Pierce was only vaguely aware of himself, floating, the euphoria of pain and stress release suspending his busy, doubting brain, putting a hold on all the words, the obstacles Pierce tended to put in his own way.

There was only peace.

"Here you go," Hal said, sitting him up. He must have gone into the other room for clothes, but Pierce didn't remember him going. "I'm going to put on your sleep shorts and your T-shirt. If you feel like dressing up later, that's fine, but until you're a little less floaty-pants, that'll do."

"Floaty-pants?" Pierce asked, bemused.

"Yeah. Dude—that euphoria thing is strong within you. I've got over 300 hours, and I don't know if I've *ever* massaged anyone that tense." He looked down, worried. "I… I wish I'd done it sooner, but you didn't seem that excited about the idea."

Pierce was too stoned on holistic pain relief to lie. About anything. "I didn't want to take advantage of you," he said baldly. "Because you're young. And pretty. And you could be spending your time with hipsters and cute college students and you spent a month making a bitter old guy feel like sunshine."

Hal paused in the middle of slipping his shorts on. "Like sunshine? No, don't get up—I'm going to put your sandals on or you're going to kill yourself on the tile."

"My feet are slippery," Pierce said wisely. Hal had spent twenty minutes on his arches and between his toes and… mmm….

"Yes, they are. I made you feel like sunshine?"

"Like the light from the sea through the sliding glass door," Pierce said, gesturing vaguely to the view. Hal had pulled back the blinds that morning, and the whole world glowed gold. "I hated it when I got here. But you make my heart feel like that. And I'm like the storm. All grim clouds. And how do I ask for more sunshine?" Pierce smiled benevolently. "I don't know how I'll even see the sun again when I can't see you."

Hal blinked hard and stood Pierce up on his sandals while wiping his eyes off on his shoulder. "That's…. God, Pierce. You're really saying these things to me. Do you even *know* what's coming out of your mouth?"

"Speaking of my mouth, are there cookies?"

Hal's laugh sounded a little bit hysterical. "Just sit here, big man, and I'm going to clean up and make you such amazing Christmas cookies, I'll ruin you for Christmas forever unless I'm there to cook for you."

"That would be amazing," Pierce said benevolently. "The having you to cook for me. And the Christmas. And the forever. I'll have to ask you sometime."

"About what?" Hal whispered, wrapping his arm around Pierce's waist.

"About forever."

"You do that," Hal said. "Whenever you're ready."

Pierce pouted. "But I'm leaving tomorrow. I'll have to text. Texting's no good. Can't smell you then. You smell like sunshine and cookies."

Hal sat him down in one of the kitchen chairs and cupped his cheeks. "You ask me whenever you're ready. Don't worry, Pierce. I'll always be there." And then he bent forward and took Pierce's mouth. For a moment the sunshine went away, and they were gliding over big fluffy clouds in a starry sky.

Not storm clouds at all.

For a moment Pierce hoped Hal could see him just like that.

And then Hal was gone, doing things with the massage table and washing his hands and starting work in the kitchen, and Pierce was left staring out into space, dreaming about a starry night above the clouds while lost in the smell of sunshine.

And cookies.

IT TOOK him about an hour to come down, and that was only because the sugar high from all the cookies gave him the kind of jolt needed to cut through all those lovely endorphins.

Finally, though, by the time dinner was done, he was completely in the moment. His body felt loose and functional, and his mind was thrilled to be following Hal's perky banter through ham and potatoes to biting the heads off the reindeer-shaped cookies and letting the headless bodies thrash around spouting pink frosting blood.

And then pelting each other with M&M's they were supposed to be using as decorations.

When they'd stopped laughing—and Hal had swept up the candy—they retreated to the living room to watch Christmas movies.

Pierce stared at *Love Actually* thoughtfully. "Weird."

"What?" Hal was a cuddler—he pushed aggressively into Pierce's arms, and Pierce wrapped himself around Hal's shoulders.

"It's... it's hard to know it's Christmas here. I mean, the stores were all decked out—and the Christmas tree helps." On one of Hal's last trips, he'd strung lights along the valance for the blinds, and that helped too.

"It's not cold enough," Hal said moodily. "Not like places that snow. I hate Florida."

"No—I mean, it's in the sixties, so it's a little warm. It's...." Pierce grimaced, feeling foolish because it had taken him a month to figure this out. "It's the sun. It's in the wrong place. And it feels like it can't be Christmas when the sun is in the wrong place."

Hal squinted up at him. "Are you still on your massage high?"

Oh God—how embarrassing. "No! It's... it's just odd. That's all. Odd."

"Sure. Whatever. Besides—tomorrow's not Christmas. It's Christmas Eve."

Pierce grunted. It felt more like D-day. "You know, you *could* just come with me to my sis—"

"Wabbit season," Hal snapped.

It was the first time they'd had to use the personal safeword that day.

"It is not," Pierce argued. "It is not Wabbit Season. Why would going to my sister's be—"

"Wabbit season," Hal insisted, scowling up at him. "We'll talk about it tomorrow."

Pierce could have pointed out the whole car situation, but he didn't. This felt bigger than having to cancel a Lyft an hour before it showed up at his door.

He squeezed Hal—hard. "You had better not disappear from my life tomorrow, you idiot duck," he muttered.

"I promise, no boom."

Pierce sat up like he'd been stung. "Was there? Was there ever going to be a boom?"

Hal rolled his eyes. "Cool your jets, panic man. I was going to *drink* myself to death—and I told you how that ended. No. There was not going to be a boom."

Pierce settled back down into the couch, but now his hands were shaking and clammy, and his pleasant Christmas doze felt shattered.

Hal sighed, took his hand, and kissed it. "Shh… it's just this night, baby. Just you and me and this movie and Christmas. Watch the movie. Hold me tight. You'll feel the Christmas thing—I promise. And the sun is exactly where it's supposed to be. I swear."

Pierce nodded, soothed by his words, by his soft kiss on the palm of Pierce's hand—and by the sweet movie that both of them quoted as it played.

"Did you hope?" Hal asked toward the middle of the movie.

"Hope for what?"

"That the guy from *Walking Dead* would find a guy instead of a girl?"

Pierce chuckled. "Well he found Daryl!"

"I meant in *this* movie."

Pierce thought about it. "No," he answered at last. "I was too busy hoping the girl with the brother didn't answer the phone."

Hal grunted. "Why?"

"Because the people you love should never get in the way of the people you love."

Hal was quiet for a moment, lying sideways with his head on Pierce's lap. "You could be the best person I've ever met," he said.

Pierce stroked his hair back from his face, his heart so full in that moment he couldn't hear the incessant crashing of the surf. "Not even close—shh… it's the part with the Dido song…."

They watched the movie, entranced, and then Hal stood up from the couch and offered him a hand up. Pierce stood, and Hal cupped his cheeks, giving him a brief kiss.

"Go undress," he said, giving orders naturally. "Pull down the duvet and lie on your side. I've got an idea."

Pierce shuddered, thinking he might know what this particular idea entailed. If he was right, it was a *good* idea, and he wanted to be a part of it.

He walked his newly loosened body into the bedroom, stripping out of his sleep shorts, boxers, and T-shirt, and unlike getting the massage, he suddenly felt *very* naked, and *very* sexual.

And in spite of the scars on his body, the silver strands of hair on his head, the lines in the corners of his green eyes, he didn't feel old and wrecked, as he had when he'd arrived here.

He felt young and desirable and in desperate need of whatever Hal wanted to dish out tonight.

He lay down on the bed on his side—not facing the end table, like Hal probably expected, but facing the center of the bed.

Hal finished turning off the lights and locking up and walked into the bedroom shucking clothes, dropping them in his usual pile next to the bed. He looked up and caught Pierce's eyes on him.

"What?"

"I was remembering that first night. In the dark. How you didn't even want to talk about it."

"I was afraid," Hal told him quietly, crawling to the middle of the bed so he could talk to Pierce eye to eye. "I wanted you so bad—so bad. But you were so... so angry. Closed off. Hurt. I thought maybe if we just kept it us, in the dark, you'd let it happen."

Pierce closed his eyes and savored how far they'd come. "I don't want you in the dark," he said. "I want... I want to walk down the street with you. I want to introduce you to everyone I know. I—"

Hal put two fingers on his lips. "I want you," he whispered. "All of you. Now roll over and turn off the light."

Pierce did, staying on his side and facing away from Hal's amber eyes.

Hal's hands—his magic hands—skated over Pierce's shoulders, his arms, his side, and Hal pressed up against Pierce's back, aggressively naked. The thought of him—all of him—lined up against Pierce's bare back sent a shiver of recognition, of arousal zinging through Pierce's body.

Hal pulled the longish hair from Pierce's ear and started talking dirty. "You like my hands?"

"Yes."

"Where do you want them?"

"Everywhere."

Hal bit his earlobe softly. "Be specific."

"Nipples," Pierce said, aware that his were tingling, needy, wanting attention in the worst way.

His was rewarded with a soft scraping of Hal's nails against the ridge of flesh, and he whined.

"Not enough?" Hal tormented.

"Pinch!"

"Sure."

But he was so greedy for the pinch, it arced through his body, electricity seeking all his erogenous zones, and he cried out and thrust his hips back and forth, immediately aching and needy.

Without prompting he propped his knee against the bed, opening his groin and his back end up for all the most exciting play he ever needed.

"Want something else?" Hal asked, laughing.

"Touch me," Pierce begged, shameless. "All the places."

"Sure."

Oh, he was wicked, this boy. He touched Pierce's flanks, the outside of his thighs, the very edge of Pierce's crease.

"You're teasing me!" Pierce accused, whimpering and not caring.

"You're being vague," Hal said, laughing. "Now be specific—"

"Stroke my c... inner thighs." Pierce loved the tantalizing touches—he would ask for them.

"Ooh—I like how you think."

Hal palmed his inner thighs, both of them, sliding the sides of his hand down the juncture of his body, feeding his wants while keeping his needs just hungry enough.

"My balls," Pierce panted. "My taint...."

"Teasing yourself!" Hal purred, thrusting up against Pierce's buttock, his cock leaving a patch of wet against Pierce's skin.

"You're doing such a good job for me!" Pierce moaned. Hal cupped his balls, scooting down a little on the bed to get access and leverage, and Pierce moaned again, breathily.

"You want more teasing?" Hal urged. "What else do you want?"

"Lick me," Pierce begged, unafraid. This was Hal—he wouldn't leave Pierce hanging. Hal moved all the way down, leaving a string of kisses down Pierce's spine. When he got to Pierce's backside, Pierce's propped knee still holding him open and accessible, he parted Pierce's cheeks and dove in.

And Pierce almost cried.

"It's so good," he panted, forgetting how this thing was supposed to work. He reached down to stroke his cock, and Hal punished him by stopping with the tongue action.

"But… but…."

"That's going to make it over too soon," Hal told him. "Just for that, roll over on your stomach."

Pierce didn't hesitate—but he *did* have to adjust himself to make sure he didn't squash his dick against the bed and tweak it forever.

Hal got between his legs, spread his cheeks, and stuck two slick fingers inside. Pierce bucked into the intrusion, driving them deeper.

"More," he begged. "Are you happy?"

Hal kept thrusting them and pulling back, and Pierce's body ached with need, hot and cold sweat popping out on his brow, on his back. Oh *God*, he needed the whole reaming act. He pulled his knees carefully under him, feeling some stiffness, some pulling on muscles, but thanks to the work he'd done this month, thanks to the massage earlier in the day, no pain.

And he sat there, spread and vulnerable, and begged the most intimate of acts from a kid he hadn't known a month ago but couldn't imagine not knowing tomorrow.

"Cocky, aren't ya?" Hal asked, thrusting his fingers in harder and faster. A cool slick drizzled down the fingers, and Hal spread it around. Pierce groaned, welcoming the stretch, the invasion, wanting more.

"You're the one with the cock," Pierce taunted back. "Are you going to do something with it?"

Hal bit his asscheek delicately, the tiny needles of pain driving Pierce higher.

"You think you're ready?" Hal asked, voice muffled in Pierce's flesh.

"I am," Pierce begged. "I am. I so am."

Hal moved from the vee of his legs. "On your side again," he ordered, then changed his voice. "It's good you can do this for a little bit now, but I don't want to take you like this—it might rip some things that just got stretched, okay?"

"Deal," Pierce mumbled, rolling to his side and propping his knee up again. "Now are you gonna—*yes*…."

There was something irrevocable about someone's cock in your ass.

Hal's cock was sized generously, but it was more than that. It was flesh inside your flesh, it was giving somebody a pass to your body and hoping they respected you enough to not hurt you.

Hal's body could have hurt, but it didn't. It filled Pierce, stretching him more, destroying his guards, the shelters Pierce had hidden in, the barriers he'd erected, swearing that he and he alone could exist behind those walls.

Hal battered them down and took their place, and Pierce cried out, not in pain, not even in pleasure, although he was aroused beyond endurance, but in surrender.

Still, Hal kept thrusting, kept *fucking*, and Pierce cried out again, gibbering, begging, needing more, and more, and more—

"*Now*," Hal panted. "*Now* you can grab your cock! C'mon, Pierce, stroke it. Squeeze it. Thumb on the top, dig it into the pee slit—that's right… tighten for me, baby. C'mon… you're almost there… oh God… you're so warm. So hot. So good. Come, baby… come for me…. *Come!*"

Pierce shouted, the orgasm contracting all his muscles, even the ones wrapped around Hal's cock. His cock spurted, his hand growing hot and sticky. Hal gave a strangled cry behind him, and Pierce felt it, Hal's spend, scalding a path inside.

Claimed. Marked. Wanted.

Pierce moaned softly as come trickled from his backside, his entire body trembling with reawakened arousal—and more.

He belonged to somebody. Somebody in his life wanted him, had staked a claim, body and soul.

The thought was annihilating—and it spiked his desire like nothing else in the world.

Hal's turn to moan, and he bit the juncture of Pierce's neck and shoulder.

"Again," Hal whispered.

"Oh God yes."

"Again," Hal chanted, snapping his hips so they bounced off Pierce's backside. His cock had hardened already, gotten, if anything, fatter and more demanding.

"Please."

"*Again!*"

And Hal fucked him hard, without mercy, without hesitation. Again.

Christmas Eve Morning

PIERCE STARED at the note, feeling again the deliciousness of his used body.

The amazing vibrancy of his reawakened heart.

He'd packed the day before, and he didn't even stop to shower before pulling on his clothes.

He wasn't sure what he was going to say, but he wanted to be wearing Hal's sex on his skin and inside his body when he said it. He barely stopped to splash water on his face and brush his teeth.

He knew which condo belonged to Hal's parents—had seen Hal disappear into it those first days—and it had always loomed, tall and unapproachable, the stairwell daunting to his wounded limbs.

The walk wasn't easy—he used his cane and the rail—but every step felt like he was ascending a tower, maybe to battle for the prince inside.

He didn't even wait to catch his breath before banging on the door.

He heard sounds inside—scurrying—the slamming of drawers and a muffled "Oh dammit!" before the door opened.

Hal stared at him, surprised and joyous.

His eyes were red rimmed, like he'd been crying.

"No," Pierce snapped, rubbing under Hal's eyes with a gentle thumb.

"No?"

"No, I'm not going to talk to you before I leave. I'm going to take you *with* me. Come with me. Don't stay here." Pierce took a deep breath, and before it could hit him that he'd said the words, he kept going. "And it's not pity. I mean, it is, but for me. Without you. Without you I'd feel so sorry for myself I'd curl up and die. I almost did, and that was before I knew you. But now that I know you—now that"—he shivered—"now that I feel you inside me, forget about it.

I can't go on. I can't go home. I can't… can't just pretend that it's Christmas unless you're there with me. Stay with me. We'll visit my sister—she'll feed you ham. We'll drive to Sacramento, and you can be a massage therapist there. I'll take you to the mountains and the ocean, where the sun's in the right place."

He paused, and Hal just gaped at him, mouth open, eyes stunned.

Pierce's voice broke. "Just stay with me. I love you. And it's stupid and idealistic, and I don't care. We can be that couple, the one who was never supposed to meet but who stayed together forever. I just know—" He took a deep shuddering breath and wiped his cheeks on his shoulders. "—I just know my life won't be good—not the job or the house or the friends or the family—none of it will be good without you in it."

He took another deep breath—or sob, actually—and wiped his eyes again, getting a good look at Hal.

Who was smiling and crying at once.

"What?" Pierce demanded. "You're just standing there—what? C'mon, say some—"

Hal opened the door and showed the two neatly packed suitcases next to him.

"Do you think I was going to let you go?" he asked. "I was gonna stalk you to Orlando and *make* you love me."

Pierce laughed, shaking, and opened his arms. Hal went—oh, so easily. He fit, like he should be there all the times forever.

"Achievement unlocked," he rasped, burying his face in Hal's hair and taking comfort from his smell. "Stalking unnecessary. Come home with me."

"Yeah."

"Be a massage therapist."

"Yeah."

"I'll love you so hard, nobody'll care that you're a kid and I'm a grown-up."

"You're not a grown-up," Hal said against his chest. "You're a unicorn."

"Unicorns are the best," Pierce agreed.

"We should know."

He'd be a unicorn for the rest of his life—forever—if it meant Hal could be there next to him, snarking, believing, playing, for every Christmas—and every day thereafter.

IT TOOK them less than an hour to be ready to leave.

Pierce locked up the condo regretfully—it had been a good home for a month. It had, in fact, been witness to some of the happiest moments of his life.

"Where're we going again?" Hal asked, checking the Lego Christmas tree carefully, surrounded in its bed of teddy bears and brightly wrapped gifts.

"Orlando," Pierce said, holding up his phone. "I've got the directions here, because I can't remember for shit."

Hal nodded, like he got that. "And afterward?"

Pierce dared him with his eyes. "North Carolina," he said, wondering if this would get him left on the curb. "To tell your parents to forward your mail to Sacramento."

Hal jerked back. "That's a terrible idea."

"Indeed it is. Gonna fight me on it?"

"Mm...." Hal gnawed that lush lower lip. "No. No—it shall be terrible and uncomfortable and irritate the crap out of them. They'll loathe you."

"Excellent. I *like* this plan!"

"And after that?" Hal prodded.

"New York," Pierce said grandly. "I've never been. I don't have to be home until February. Let's enjoy this shit."

A dreamy smile took over Hal's face. "Really? Adventures?"

"Two knights riding a CR-V unicorn," Pierce told him grandly.

"Two unicorns with opposable thumbs," Hal corrected.

"We'll conquer the world," Pierce decided, hopping in the car and getting this road on the show.

He slammed the door with a satisfying thunk, and Hal hopped in and hit the ignition.

"As long as in the end we end up in the same stable." Hal's eyes were big and limpid amber, and Pierce got it.

"Yeah, unicorn," he said gently, squeezing Hal's knee. "There's home at the end of the rainbow. I promise."

Hal's face lit up, like he'd needed to hear it one more time. "Then into the great wide yonder it is!" He gestured grandly into the unexpectedly bright, crisp day, and hit the ignition.

They had relatives to visit and cookies to bake and grand adventures before them.

And a life together at the end of the quest.

There had never been happier unicorns.

Pierce and Hal's Road Trip

INTRODUCTION

OKAY, SO structurally *Regret Me Not* was perfect. It had the perfect plot arc for a Christmas story and the perfect ride-off-into-the-sunset ending.

But I wasn't ready to say goodbye.

I had so many moments for these guys after they left Florida—they were all mapped out in my head, all beautiful. But they just didn't fit the story.

So I talked to Lynn, my editor-in-chief-who-should-be-nominated-for-sainthood, and said, "Hey, how about if I put those moments on my blog, and then we add them to the text. That way we can release a paperback before Christmas next year!" (Although the bulk of my sales are in e-book, I have a terrible fetish for seeing my stuff in paperback. I can't even explain it, except that I think it makes me old.)

She said sure, even though this is a giant pain in the ass for her, and I owe her too much knitting to ever finish.

But she said sure.

So here are the further adventures of Pierce and Hal in their quirky, painful, weird, and wonderful glory.

They eat magical food and meet magical people and, every day, fall more in love.

I hope you fall more in love with them as well.

CHAPTER 1
GUIDING STAR

"HUH," HAL said skeptically as he piloted his CR-V through the little suburban street.

"You sound disappointed."

"And you sound tired." Hal gave him a once-over at the light. The house was small and unassuming, and Hal wondered what he was doing here when so much about him was big and assuming a lot.

But Pierce's family was here, and he loved them, and Hal loved Pierce, and family was always sort of a test, right?

Hal really wanted to pass this test.

They'd talked nonstop from Tampa to Orlando, making plans, tentative timetables, hotel arrangements. Pierce was pretty handy with his phone, and Hal was forced to remember he was a computer engineer with lots of business cred under his belt. He'd certainly organized their next month and a half to within an inch of its life.

But they'd agreed—they'd mapped out the trip, they knew how long they were staying at Sasha's and about how long it would take them to get to Hal's parents, and even had reservations for a week in New York City.

Pierce wanted to see the statue, and Hal wanted to see *Hamilton*, and Pierce wasn't sure he could get those tickets, but they had almost a month, so he said he'd try.

Pierce, excited and planning their journey in the seat next to him, wasn't any less wonderful than he had been when he'd ventured up the stairs to knock on the door and ask Hal to come with him forever.

But now they were here, at an average-sized suburban house, green, with a shady oak tree in the front yard and probably a pool in the back. Possibly an alligator in the pool—Hal had always hoped to see one.

But he was more excited about Pierce, green eyes fluttering closed, reddish-toned brown hair flat against his head as he fought off the effects of an eventful morning—and a really awesome night.

"Pierce? We're here."

Pierce sat up quickly and winced, then gave a self-conscious smile. "Here. Let's get the presents out, and my overnight bag and one of your suitcases—"

"Here, Uncle Pierce," Hal said with a wink. "Let me get the presents out, and you can go say hi to that scary woman with the apron and the spoon." Her hair was a mane of curls—thank you, Florida, because nobody was safe—and the spoon was covered in cookie dough, and Hal sort of loved her already.

"Sasha!" Pierce's face lit up like Hal had seen when he'd been on the phone, and he had a moment's wistfulness for siblings he'd never been granted. He got out creakily, and Hal hesitated. Did he need help? Would he stumble? A month of watching Pierce rehabilitate himself from someone wiped out by an hour in the water to somebody who could make it through almost a whole day, and Hal still had moments of panic:

This person spoke to Hal's heart in a way no man ever had. God, let him be okay.

But Hal needn't have worried.

Sasha was small but just as fine-boned as her tall, lanky brother. Pierce wrapped long arms around her shoulders and hugged her tight, and she waved the spoon over her head so she didn't get gunk on him.

"You made it! We started without you—I hope that's okay!"

Pierce pulled back and smiled, part of his mouth twisting higher than the other as he bit his lip self-consciously. "Is that cookie dough? 'Cause if that's cookie dough, I want that."

Sasha had a gamine little smirk, the counterpart to her brother's goofy grin. "It's amazing," she promised and gave Pierce probably four hundred calories of cookie dough in one swallow.

His eyes actually rolled back in his head, and Hal decided that yes, he'd be fine while Hal got the luggage.

"Wait!" Pierce said, disentangling himself. "Here—let me help. At least let me bear the gifts!"

Hal chuckled, and Pierce grinned, and for a moment they were just them. "Yeah, yeah," Pierce filled in, "since we know your gift is a bear...."

Hal let loose an actual laugh and met Sasha's smiling face. "I can get it all," he said, but Sasha shook her head.

"Nope. You're a guest too." She turned toward the still-open front door and cranked her voice up to mom volume with a single inhale. "Kids! Marshall! Come help get stuff! Pierce needs to go inside."

Pierce grimaced. "I'm really much better—I swear, Sash, I didn't just curl up and die there."

"I can vouch for that." Hal pulled the last of the bags out, making a tidy little pile on the lawn. "Swimming, walks—the works. He was a good boy."

"Well, he always was," Sasha said softly. Behind them, a tiny herd of elephants clattered across the porch and down the stairs, and Hal lost Sasha and Pierce as a medium-sized man and two smallish children came tumbling across the yard.

Fifteen minutes later the kids had carried the gifts and put them under the tree and Marshall had helped Hal with the bags to the tiny guest room with a queen-sized bed.

"You'll both be staying here, right?" Marshall was a completely average Caucasian man—brown hair, hazel eyes, skin that would tan with sunblock and burn without. But he didn't bat an eyelash when he asked that question, and Hal was a fan.

"Yes—thank you."

"So, Sasha said a week, right? We've been looking forward to Pierce's visit—I hope that's okay."

"Yeah—we're moving on to my parents' the day after New Years—we sort of put together a schedule."

Marshall laughed and looked behind his shoulder, like he was imparting a secret. "Look, between you and me? Don't let him get too hooked on his schedule, okay? This thing with you? That's as spontaneous as I've ever seen Pierce. Keep it up!"

And Hal had a friend.

An hour later, Pierce and Sasha and Marshall were all talking in the kitchen about jobs and markets and things that made Hal's eyes glaze over. He stole a couple of cookies and wandered into the front room, where Darius and Abigail were playing with their own Legos and looking with awe and respect at the Lego tree Hal had made from random blocks.

"Did you make this?" Darius demanded. "I don't see the schematics!"

"I made up the design myself," Hal said smugly. "Want to do another one with me?" Because he still had Legos in *his* box.

"Yes!" It was unanimous, and an hour later Pierce wandered out of the kitchen, moving slowly. Hal turned and patted the couch cushion behind him.

"Here—sit down," he said, trying not to fuss. Their whole relationship had been built on him cheerleading instead of fussing. But now there were people—kind, beautiful people, but other people—who didn't seem to be cheerleading him in the right spots. He should have been urged to sit in the kitchen. Maybe a lie-down before all the socializing. They'd stopped to eat on the way, but all the sugar wasn't good for—

"I've got some veggies and bean dip," Pierce said softly. "There's more in the kitchen, but you disappeared." He held out the plate, and Hal took it gratefully. Building Legos was hard work.

"Look, Uncle Pierce!" Darius cried. "Hal's been teaching us how to make trees! Mine has pirate heads for decoration!"

Pierce snorted. "That's amazing, D. I think you should show your mother that—she'll be so excited!"

"Mine has shoes!" Abigail cried, not to be outdone. Hal beamed at her. She'd pulled out an entire box full of Barbie shoes, and he'd helped her run sewing thread through them and put them up as tiny ornaments too.

"That's truly amazing," Pierce agreed. "Go show your mom, and then they said we could watch some TV."

The kids got up and disappeared, and Pierce sighed and sank back into the couch. "Get up here with me," he said softly.

"Why?" But Hal was already scooping the Legos into piles and putting them away.

"Because I miss you. I know we got all involved, but I didn't mean to drive you out of the kitchen."

Hal finished scooping Legos and stood up, plate of bean dip in hand. In the other room, he could hear the kids chattering excitedly and being rewarded with cookies.

His irritation disappeared, and he sank gratefully into the couch with Pierce. "Your family is nice," he said, but that seemed inadequate. The kids had been a charming disaster, squabbling, one-upping—but also playing. Helping. Darius had praised the shoe idea to the skies. Abigail had helped him decapitate fifteen Lego pirates.

"I wasn't ready to leave our little bubble," Pierce told him, leaning against his shoulder. "I had you to myself for a month. It was heavenly."

It was… it was exactly how Hal felt.

"Your family loves you," Hal said as graciously as he could, remembering Sasha and the cookie dough and Marshall telling him not to plan and the kids getting excited because Uncle Pierce's presents were the best.

"You love me," Pierce murmured. "That's still magic, you know. We just said those words this morning."

And the disappointment at seeing the small suburban house faded away. The alienation of the grown-up talk about jobs and income and taxes melted away. That feeling—that terrible feeling of being exiled from his lover's side to the kids' table—it was like it had never existed.

"And you love me," Hal said, because he was right. The words were magic. And some magic spells had to be repeated before the magic became fully real.

"Course." Pierce snuggled against him. "The Barbie shoes were classic, by the way."

"All your niece."

"Heh, heh—all Sasha."

But as Pierce's breathing got even and he sank into a much-needed nap, Hal had to wonder. For all Marshall's warning, Hal had seen Pierce play, had seen him be spontaneous. Maybe the pirate heads and the Barbie shoes were a quiet gift from Pierce as well, just nobody saw it but Hal.

The thought gave Hal another layer of warmth for the man practically lying in his arms.

He melted into the couch a little more, finishing off the veggies and putting the plate on the end table so he could wrap an arm around Pierce's shoulder.

By the time the kids came out, Pierce was asleep against his chest, and he didn't stir when the kids turned on cartoon Christmas specials.

Hal was completely immersed in *How the Grinch Stole Christmas!* when Darius and Abigail crawled onto the couch too, Darius on one side of him, Abigail in his lap. For a moment he sat, stunned, wondering why a child might possibly do such a thing.

But he remembered that Pierce loved these children, and they'd welcomed him when he'd been uncertain.

An hour later Sasha came out and had everybody wash up for dinner. The kids were put to bed a few hours later, with snacks and hugs and Pierce reading "'Twas the Night Before Christmas" with just enough drama for Hal to wonder if he'd ever dreamed of being on stage.

And finally they were alone together, in the tiny bed in the tiny guest room, listening to the unfamiliar noises in the unfamiliar house.

"Pierce?"

"Mm?"

"What if we want to change the schedule?"

"Okay."

"You're not going to ask how?"

"No." He sounded tired.

"You're not curious?"

The chuckle in the dark reassured him. "I'm very curious," Pierce said, propping himself up on his good arm and facing Hal. "I mean, the kids sat down with plain old Legos and came out with pop art masterpieces. What can you do with an atlas and a cell phone? I wait in awe."

Hal smirked. "But some of that was you!" he protested. "Those kids were bent long before I got here."

"I have no idea what you're talking about," Pierce declared airily. "I never watched *Coraline* with them when their mother said no, and I certainly never played pirate execution last Easter when I was down here for a visit."

Hal frowned then, because Pierce had still been married. "Did Cynthia let you do that?" Oh, Hal didn't like his ex-wife.

"No," Pierce said, voice sober. "Because I asked her not to come."

"Because why?"

"Because, baby. This is my family. And I know they're a little bit suburban and boring to you—but I don't let anybody near them I don't trust. And I was starting not to trust her by then."

Oh! And this made it all worth it. "But you trust me?"

"Very much. You were…" Even in the dark, Hal could see Pierce's face go soft. "Amazing. After you left, we must have paused half a dozen times just to hear you play."

Not exiled to the kids' table. Not forgotten. Listened to. Appreciated. Trusted.

Hal had to swallow against the lump in his throat. He kissed Pierce instead, openmouthed, carnally, because it was Christmas Eve, dammit, and all he'd wanted for Christmas for his whole life was a Pierce.

They necked, kissing fiercely, until Pierce pulled away, grimacing. "Uh… Hal?"

"You don't want to have sex in your sister's house on Christmas Eve?"

"Do you mind?"

"No. But it might cut our stay short. Do you mind?"

Pierce's teeth glinted in the dark. "Do I mind that you want sex with me? No. No, I don't mind that at all."

"But it will kill your schedule."

"I already said that's okay."

"But how will you know when to stick to the schedule and when not to?"

Pierce spread his hand on the base of Hal's throat, almost a Neanderthal move from a guy who'd been willing to follow. "You're my star, Hal. I'll follow you. I can't go wrong that way, you think?"

"I'm your star?" Oh Jesus. His throat practically closed up.

"Yeah. My guiding star out of mediocrity and complete averageness."

"So… your schedule, your phone—I'm more important?" As he'd never been to his parents. Either of them.

"Didn't we cover this idea this morning?" Pierce asked, swallowing a yawn. "The whole I love you? Save me from myself? If my self isn't on the track that gets sex with you, then by all means save me!"

Hal pushed gently at his shoulder. "Shift over," he ordered, "so I can spoon you." Because Hal was the bossiest and got to be big spoon.

"Fine." Pierce yawned again. "Is this a magic Christmas spoon that's as good as sex? Because you kissed me and got me all het up."

"And you didn't offer so much as a hand job, you prudish bastard." Pierce rolled over, and Hal wrapped his arm around his middle, squeezing tightly. "And it is a magic Christmas spoon that's as good as sex, because you are a magic Christmas unicorn, and just being with you is Christmas even when I'm exiled to the kiddie Lego room and you get to talk about death and taxes with the grown-ups."

"You know, you left early. How do you know we didn't start talking about cartoons and Disney World?"

"Please. If you'd said one word about Disney World, those two lovely, angelic children would have been all over your ass with bribery and blackmail."

Pierce chuckled softly. "Well, maybe we can come back sometime and take them."

Hal kissed him between the shoulder blades and settled down to being sexless but Pierce-ful for the next seven days. "I'll do that," he said, not because he couldn't live without kids like Pierce apparently couldn't, but because he was invited and trusted and appreciated.

And because he was Pierce's guiding star, and Pierce loved his family. Hal vowed never to steer him away from them, because this moment here was maybe the best Christmas he'd ever had.

CHAPTER 2
NUN'S DILEMMA

HAL LOVED Pierce's little sister, Sasha, especially after spending a week with her and her adorable family over Christmas.

But he really hated her tiny suburban house.

"What are you—"

He flailed. "Sh!" He glared at Sasha, and her hazel-green eyes—so much like her brother's—widened. "He's talking," he mouthed, hoping she'd catch on.

"To who?" To her credit, she didn't raise her voice, but she did raise her eyebrows.

"Cynthia," Hal whispered.

And now Sasha's eyes got really big. "Because why?"

Hal grimaced. Pierce had told him that New Year's Eve was his and Cynthia's thing, and in the interest of being amicable exes, he'd promised he'd call her this New Years, just to say hi.

Hal personally thought she was a big ol' moo, and he'd just as soon she kept her bitchy self away from Pierce, because the guy had been pretty beaten down when Hal had found him, and as far Hal could see, Cynthia was most of the reason.

But then Pierce was a much better grown-up than Hal had ever been, so Hal was going to trust his judgment on this one.

Sort of.

"Mom! Where's Uncle Pierce!"

It was fun to watch Sasha flail this time as she tried to keep her oldest, Darius, from running into the bedroom where Pierce was talking quietly.

"Ooolf! Hello, big man!" Pierce said, surprised. He still wasn't recovered 100 percent from his car wreck, but Hal had forced him around the block a couple of times a day, and he peeked into the room and made sure that Pierce was still standing. "Where's your mom?"

"She and Uncle Hal are standing outside the doorway making faces at each other, but you're leaving tomorrow and you promised to play Monopoly until it's New Years or until I fell asleep—remember? One or the other. You promised."

"Sure. I'll be out in a minute. Tell Uncle Hal that I'm fine and he can stop eavesdropping now."

Hal scowled at Sasha, who chuckled back. "Small house," she said cheerfully. "Thin walls."

"Whatever," he mumbled, embarrassed. "I wasn't eavesdropping!" he called before entering the room. Pierce was sitting on the bed, one arm around Darius, closing up the conversation.

"Yeah, Cynthia—sorry—I gotta go. Apparently the world will end if I don't play Monopoly." His usual dry humor suddenly disappeared, and the expression on his angular, arresting features became sober. "You're welcome, honey. I hope this year is better for both of us. Yeah. You too. Night."

"So can we go?" Darius demanded, and Pierce ruffled his hair.

"You go first and set up the game. I need to talk to Hal for a second, okay?"

"God, grown-ups suck," Darius grumbled—but he got up and headed for the door. He rounded the corner and shouted, "Abi! You've got to set up the game or Uncle Pierce won't play!", leaving Hal and Pierce snickering in the aftermath.

Hal met Pierce's eyes and Pierce held out his arm.

God, he was warm. Hal snuggled into him, wrapping his arms around Pierce's waist and leaning his head on a sharp shoulder.

"You've got nothing to be worried about," Pierce said mildly. "She just wanted to touch base. You know—seven years is a long time to leave somebody cold."

"She could have made you feel like shit," Hal grumbled.

"Well, I could have too—"

"No, you couldn't. You're too decent."

Pierce chuckled mirthlessly. "You know that's not true."

"Whatever. I don't care. What does 'You too' mean?"

Pierce stiffened. "Wow, you really were listening!"

"Seriously—what was that a response to?"

Pierce sighed and tightened his arm. "She said 'I love you, Pierce. Take care,' and I said, 'You too.'"

Hal breathed in and breathed out. It had been a risk, taking Pierce up on his offer of love, his "Come with me. I love you. Let's be together." Even after a really nice week visiting with Pierce's sister, it was still hard to believe Pierce was all his.

"Do you?" he asked, hating himself. "Still love her?"

Pierce breathed in and out, weighing the question. "I'm trying to, but only as a friend. I swear."

Gah! "So, you know how tomorrow we were going to drive balls-out and get to my parents', right?"

"Yeah?"

"Well, how about we drive balls-out to Atlanta, which has a great theater scene and restaurants and some really cool historical sites, and spend three days there having all the sex in the world, and then drive to my parents' in Charlotte?"

Pierce's low chuckle told him he wasn't fooled in the least. "You're stalling," he sang.

"Se-ex!" Hal sang back insistently.

"Well, since we've been here a week and have remained chaste as a nun's dreams—"

"That you know of."

"That I know of. Sure. I think we need to have some—"

Hal captured his mouth in a hard, forget-me-not kind of kiss.

Because Pierce got him. And would let him put off talking to his parents. And wouldn't lie to him about being in love with his ex.

And still wanted all the sex in the world.

Hal had to break the kiss off because Pierce was clinging to him raggedly, breathing hard. "Okay. So. Atlanta. Has a great theater scene," he panted.

"Smashing," Hal agreed, although he'd only heard this and hadn't seen anything himself.

"We'll never see it."

"Never," Hal said, taking his mouth again.

Pierce groaned throatily and pulled back. "Monopoly," he begged, and Hal conceded, only because it had been a week and if they didn't get up and go play Monopoly now they might break their "Oh my God it's Pierce's sister's house and she has kids and what kind of monsters are we?" abstinence.

But Hal still heard the promise. Pierce had just broken up with a wife who'd made him hate himself for seven years and could still say sincerely, "Love you back, take care." Hal was going to be the spouse who made him feel wonderful about himself for the rest of his life. Hal could live with a return on that investment. In fact, he planned to.

CHAPTER 3
SNAKES ON THE ROAD

"Is it over?" Hal sounded peevish—and, for one of the rare times in their relationship, young.

"Is what over? I'm not looking either, remember?" But Pierce definitely sounded like a grumpy bastard.

"Oh Jesus. They climb up through the engine. I read that once. They can climb out of the ventilation at any time."

Pierce recoiled. He'd seen that meme too. "I hate you so much."

"I was going to offer you a blow job to pass the time."

For a moment Pierce forgot his fear and looked at Hal curiously, and Hal looked back, his magnificent amber eyes wide. Then they both clapped their hands over their eyes.

"*Oh* holy trouser snakes, *no!*" Pierce snapped.

"I may never have sex again," Hal said, sounding haunted. "I'm twenty-three. Those are some of my best years."

"We *will* have sex again!" Pierce said with determination. "But first…."

"One of us has to open his eyes."

They took a deep breath in tandem, and Pierce felt Hal's hand creep into his own. They laced their fingers together, and Pierce said, "Okay. On three. One, two, three, *look!*"

"*Auuuuuuuughhhhhhhh!*"

"*There's more of them!*"

"Oh Jesus God," Hal moaned. "We're going to die here. We're going to be the skeleton in *Indiana Jones* with the snakes coming out of the eyeballs."

"I hate you." Pierce thought he was going to throw up.

"But… but you love me too, right?" Sudden vulnerability. Pierce opened his eyes and looked determinedly at Hal and only at Hal and not at the road in front of them.

"Yeah, baby. I still love you."

"Even though I took the wrong turn into the state park with the snake migration?"

Pierce breathed deeply. "It's going to make a great story. Just as soon as…."

"Yeah. As soon as the goddamned snakes stop crossing the road."

CHAPTER 4
SEX SEASON

THE TRIP to Atlanta took more than ten hours, because fuck Atlanta and fuck traffic and fuck snakes in Georgia, that's why. By the time they made it into the hotel room—the really super nice hotel room Pierce had booked for them New Years morning, because he apparently hadn't figured out that he had the job yet and was still trying to impress Hal when Hal was doing the exact same thing—Pierce could barely move.

They'd stopped for food after the unfortunate snake incident, so as soon as Hal could get Pierce prone, he stripped off his clothes, grabbed some towels, and started to work on the muscles that had frozen in transit. After an hour of hard labor—because being a masseur wasn't for the weak of heart or of hand—the tight lines of agony had released Pierce's jaw, and a couple of ibuprofen helped with some of the residual pain. But they were exhausted by then, and the most Hal could manage was some television, while Pierce mumbled about snakes and cowboys as he wandered to sleep.

The next morning, Hal woke up from a sound slumber to hear Pierce in the shower, singing. He fell back asleep, and when he woke up again, there was a flat of coffees and a bag of pastries next to the bed and Pierce was feathering a kiss along Hal's temple.

"Look who's all bright and shiny," Hal mumbled. "Last night you could barely move."

"Yeah, but I know a guy with really awesome hands," Pierce purred, his breath tracing a path down Hal's jaw, down his neck, down his shoulder.

"I do have awesome hands, don't I," Hal conceded. He rolled to his back and kicked off the covers, inviting Pierce to kiss anywhere else he wanted.

What he wanted was to pull Hal's nipple into his mouth and suck.

"Nungh!" Hal's fingers tangled in Pierce's overlong red-brown hair, and his body threatened to come off the bed. "Gah!"

Pierce *hmm*ed around his nipple and teased slightly with his teeth, and Hal's entire body sang.

Oh God.

He'd finally found a man whose touch made him feel like a real person, a whole man who could give and receive pleasure without pain or uncertainty, and they'd spent the last week cuddling.

His penis woke up and declared cuddling illegal and demanded all things carnal right now.

"Pierce!" Hal gasped, arching his hips up, and Pierce let go of his nipple and kept kissing down.

"Are we impatient?" he asked, toying with the waistband to Hal's pricey satin boxers.

"If you suck my dick now, you can have my soul for all of eternity," Hal told him in complete earnestness.

Pierce chuckled and nudged at his hips. "Scoot over, soulless minion. I'll take you up on that offer, but I need room on the bed."

Hal did, and before Pierce could entertain any notions about teasing or trying to prolong the sex, Hal stripped off his boxers, because there was no reason to prolong something they were going to have nonstop for three days.

"You take all the mystery out of things," Pierce accused, settling his stiff body carefully so he could support his weight on his good shoulder and hold Hal in his other hand.

"Fuck mystery," Hal breathed. "Fuck mystery, fuck seduction. Just blow me now, and next time I can, you know...."

"Fuck me...," Pierce whispered, his breath skating over Hal's damp cockhead and amping the whole thing up some more.

"I'll stretch you out so sweet," Hal promised, eyes closing dreamily. It took some work, because Pierce was still in recovery, but the results... God. He'd never had a lover so boneless, so accepting, so welcoming.

All the preparation was worth it. Just thinking about it made Hal harder, and oh God, Pierce's fingers were squeezing him just so, and his breath was hot and his tongue....

Hal gasped, shoulders coming off the mattress as Pierce plied his perfectly functioning tongue over his tip, his base, his frenulum, his slit.... Oh God. Oh hell. Hal pressed the soles of his feet against the nice sheets and fought coming off the mattress entirely.

"Pierce...," he breathed. "Please. Oh God. Please...."

Pierce engulfed him, taking him all the way into the back of his throat, and he cried out, and then again as Pierce squeezed his base and pulled his head up, letting Hal slide out until just his lips engulfed the bell.

And again, and again, and again, and that's all it took before Hal screamed and came completely apart, tugging hard at Pierce's hair as he convulsed in orgasm.

Pierce pulled off him, slurping gently, and rested his head against Hal's thigh. He gave Hal a dreamy smile and held out his hand to lace fingers together.

"You look really pleased with yourself, old man," Hal panted. God, he loved Pierce when he was confident. He loved him falling apart and loved him when he was a crotchety old curmudgeon too, but he was just so beautiful when he smiled like that, like he knew how to love and be loved in return.

"I just made my young lover come," Pierce said simply. "I'm a little proud."

"You should be. You should watch me gloat when we do what I've got planned tonight. It's gonna be major."

Pierce chuckled. "The sex or the gloating?"

"Both."

"Fantastic. I've often said I was missing the erotic possibilities of a good gloat."

Hal giggled, because he was naked and replete, and he'd just had an orgasm before coffee.

"Well stay tuned for a romantic experience," he intoned, pushing up against the headboard and dislodging Pierce enough to make him sit up. "Now, are you going to help me with breakfast?"

"Sure," Pierce said. "But I'm going to drag a chair over here because—"

"Wait, no, I'll get it!"

Oh God. Hal forgot sometimes. All the time. Pushing through to Atlanta the day before had been his awesome sucktastic idea. He couldn't forgive himself for the pain that had etched itself along Pierce's mouth. He vaulted over the bed naked and grabbed the desk chair, shoved it around so Pierce could sit next to him with breakfast on the end table.

"Hal—" Pierce sighed—then laughed, probably because Hal's junk was flapping as he flailed about the room. "Okay, fine. Thank you." With a sigh he pushed up from the bed using his cane and eased himself gingerly down onto the chair. "You know, there's some drawbacks to this road trip I hadn't anticipated."

Hal was busy pulling on his pajamas so he could scramble back into the bed and eat his breakfast. "Yeah. I really do think three days here is going to be necessary. You'll need to be as loose as possible before we go visit my parents."

Pierce nodded. "Should I make reservations—"

"Yes," Hal said without hesitating. "Trust me, Pierce. I'd love to let you stay there—they've got a spa with a Jacuzzi and a big pool. All the shit I'd like to let you spoil yourself with. But no. My parents will make you long for a bed of nails and a big granite slab before you spend the night there. Trust me."

Pierce grimaced in that way that said, "I do trust you, but you're young, and we can't both have lost in the parent lottery, right?"

And Hal might have bridled at that once, but Pierce was already pulling out his phone and setting up reservations for Charlotte, and Hal had to concede. Pierce did trust him.

Hal reached out as he was surfing his travel app and cupped Pierce's cheek.

"What?" Pierce looked up and caught his hand.

"We can skip my parents," he said softly. "We can skip my parents and go to New York and see plays there and shave three days off our trip so we can get you home."

Pierce smiled slightly. "I'm not ready to go home. It's travel season. We're on a honeymoon."

Hal grinned. "Yeah, you are. Someday there might even be a wedding."

"There'll be a season for that too. Now eat. Eat, and we can go exploring and come back and use the pool."

"And then more sex?"

"Like I said—it's sex season."

Hal chuckled as dirty as he could. "My favorite time of year."

CHAPTER 5
DUCK SEASON

PIERCE HAD to admit—Hal's parents' place was pretty damned intimidating.

The long drive from the main road to the gigantic antebellum house was paved, thank God, because Pierce's body had pretty much decided travel was the suck. The three days they'd spent in Atlanta had helped, as had Hal's insistence on using the Jacuzzi and the pool while they were there, so Pierce thought maybe, with some more attention to stopping every two hours, he could make the trip home.

His other option was to give Hal directions to drive by himself while Pierce flew, and he really didn't want to do that. Even if he was sitting in the passenger seat, watching the unfamiliar scenery whiz by as Hal negotiated the expressways, listening as Hal sang loudly to pop songs Pierce had never heard of, Pierce was as happy as he'd ever been in his life.

He didn't have to be home until mid-February, and his ex-wife was setting up the bedroom and the backyard for him, like he'd asked when she'd sent the divorce papers. He was bringing Hal to a proper home. Hal had seriously left everything behind him—parents, school, friends—so he could start a life with a guy he'd known for a month. Pierce really didn't want him to regret that.

Seeing this long driveway and the spectacular house didn't bode well for Hal not regretting things.

"Damn," he muttered.

"It looks like a prison?" Hal asked.

"It looks awesome. How was it a prison?"

Hal grunted. "Do you see the house next door?"

Pierce peered through the beech trees that lined the driveway and saw nothing but rolling horse pasture crisscrossed with wooden fences. "No. I think there's a barn about half a mile away."

"That's a whole mile. We've got a golf cart to take us out to the barn. Anyway, no, there were no next-door neighbors. There were no play dates. There were no other kids invited to come sit in the living room and watch movies."

Pierce grunted. His parents had been cold and detached as well—but the house he'd grown up in would fit in this house's living room. "Me neither," he said. "I did have soccer, though. What'd you have?"

"Boarding school."

Pierce let out a little sigh. "Do you want kids?" he asked out of the blue.

"Someday, yes," Hal said, slowing down and glancing at him. "Is that a problem?"

"No. Just, you know. We need to make plans. Soccer teams and swim parties and trips to the zoo. We can take turns working from home."

Hal smiled softly, his entire oval-shaped, boy-beautiful face lighting up. "We can spoil our kids like your sister spoiled hers."

His sister's house was tiny. That Hal thought Darius and Abigail were spoiled told Pierce everything he needed to know. "Yup. And all of that will start with you telling your parents where you're moving to."

"Deal."

Still, when an older man with thinning white hair over a liver-spotted pink scalp came out to greet them and park the car, Pierce couldn't help but be impressed.

"Thanks, Daniel," Hal said kindly. "I thought you'd retired."

"Your mother seems to think she can't abide without me, sir." Daniel smiled creakily, his dentures a shining white. "And I'd be bored if I didn't at least park the cars, even if driving full-time is a little much for me."

"Well, as long as you're happy," Hal told him dubiously. "But seriously—you can always tell my parents no."

"I don't know why." Daniel laughed. "You've done so enough for the both of us!"

Hal chuckled and came around to help Pierce out of the car. Pierce was about to shake him off when, to his embarrassment, his leg buckled.

"Oh, oh…." Hal clucked, wrapping his arm around Pierce's waist and forcing Pierce to give him some of his weight. "We drove too long, didn't we?"

"I'm fine," Pierce said softly. "Just take my elbow up to the porch and I'll be fine."

Hal grunted. "I'll make sure we get you seated as soon as we get inside, okay?"

How embarrassing. "Sure."

But apparently getting up the stairs wasn't the only trial he had in store for him this day.

A butler (butler!) opened the large french door to the right and ushered them inside, where a midsized slender woman stood wearing a winter-white pant suit, her dyed ice-blonde hair twisted up into a fashionable coif. Her face was flawlessly—if heavily—made up, and she smiled thinly and offered her cheek for Hal to kiss. "Harold."

"Hi, Mom. This is Pierce—I was hoping we could—"

"Dinner isn't for another hour, Harold. Are you planning to stay the night?"

"No. I didn't think about dinner—we can be out of here by then. I just wanted you to meet—"

"Well, you must certainly stay for dinner. I'll have your room prepared, just in case." She eyed Pierce up and down, like fish for dinner. "Where will your friend be staying? We can have Daniel drive him there."

"I'm staying with him. I'll drive us fine."

Pierce smiled greenly at her disdainfully raised eyebrow. "I'm, uh, Pierce Atwater." He stuck his hand out gamely, holding desperately on to the cane with his other hand. "I've been traveling with Hal—"

"I've been traveling with you," Hal interrupted. "My car, your destination."

Pierce smiled at him, their eye contact feeling like an oasis in the middle of an emotional desert. "Yeah, but you drive. I'm pretty sure I'm just along for the ride."

Hal's smile, as subdued as it was, seemed to give color and warmth to this sterile white-marbled hallway. No wonder Hal was so irrepressible. He'd had to shine hard and long to even make this house livable for someone who needed color and kindness. "I'll give you a ride anytime, sailor," he said with a quietly bawdy wink.

Pierce winked back. "Anyway," he continued, pulling his eyes away from Hal's extraordinary amber gaze, "Hal and I have reservations in Charlotte. It's barely an hour away."

"Indeed," she said, the disapproval rolling off her like a wave. "Well, it's good you have reservations, Mr. Atwater, but I wouldn't count on Harold accompanying you. He does start school next week."

"No, I don't," Hal said, exchanging a panicked look with Pierce. "Mom, I called you the day after Christmas. I told you I wasn't going back."

"Nonsense."

"No, seriously—Pierce and I are driving to his house in California!"

"For all you know, he lives in a homeless shelter, Harold—don't be ridiculous."

"It's a house," Pierce said quietly.

"Mom, I wanted you to meet him."

"And so I have." Her tone left Pierce under no delusions as to his importance or impressiveness.

"I wanted Dad to meet him."

"He'll be down for dinner. I doubt Mr. Atwater will want to remain."

"Well, if he goes, I go. I'm a fully grown adult, and I told you what my plan was. Why can't you just believe—?"

"Harold Justice Lombard, who leaves a college education and a hefty inheritance to go be... what? A masseur in California? Do people even run away to California anymore? What, are you going to give massages on the beach?"

"I live in Sacramento," Pierce said, because talking to himself was fun. "It's two hours from the beach." His leg ached fiercely, and his hip wasn't far behind. Hal had tried—he really had given it his best to get Pierce to the living room, but his mother had pretty much cornered them in the foyer.

"I have enough of my own money to get a license," Hal argued, and it was the plan they had come up with together. "A year working for a reputable place and I can start taking clients of my own."

"Clients." She rolled her slightly protuberant eyes. "Harold, you're barely old enough to inherit your money—"

"But I am old enough. Mother, we didn't have to come here. I was all for skipping Charlotte and driving to New York. Can you not even shake his hand?"

"I'm not going to know him long enough to bother!" she snapped, and then Pierce snapped too. Or rather his abused body gave a shiver and a fail, and he almost fell to the floor.

"Fuck!" Hal snapped, wrapping his arm more securely around Pierce's waist. "Mother, I'm taking him to the living room. He needs to sit somewhere not the car, and then we need to leave."

Wonderful. But Hal's hand on his hip was exquisitely gentle, and the look he shot Pierce was full of remorse.

"It's not your fault," Pierce said softly as they walked down the hall and then to the right, into a sitting room that really was the size of the house Pierce had grown up in. "You tried to warn me."

"Yeah," Hal grumbled, "but you were trying to be a good guy."

"Maybe your father will be a better sell?"

But no, Harold Justice Lombard the Fourth was not an easier sell. After sitting for an hour in icy silence, punctuated only by Hal's running to the kitchen to fetch them some water and ibuprofen so Pierce could hydrate and wouldn't start cramping, a bell rang from somewhere else in the first floor. Hal's mother stood and clicked her way across the marble tile floors in two-inch taupe heels while Hal guided a barely refreshed Pierce to the dining room.

Once they got there, they stood at the long table, waiting for….

"What are we waiting for?" Pierce asked, knuckles white on the back of the really uncomfortable-looking wooden chair.

"My father needs to come down," Hal said. His utter disgust indicated that this wasn't a joke, and then he looked sharply at his mother. "Mother, Pierce is sitting down." With that, he pulled the chair out slightly and helped Pierce down before moving to stand behind his own chair.

"Sit down with me," Pierce said.

Hal looked at him, and looked at his mother, and then looked at the doorway that led from the staircase to the bedrooms. He looked at Pierce again, and Pierce could watch him do the math. His father was leaving them to wait—which was a dick move in any household, but apparently this one made it especially douchey. And Hal had just defied his mother as it was. With a scowl in her direction, he sat down next to Pierce, and they both took a look at the covered dishes placed around the table.

"What do you think's in them?" Pierce asked idly, unable to take the silence anymore. Fuck it, actually—he couldn't hate anybody more thoroughly after an hour of acquaintance as he hated Hal's mother. If Hal was really leaving with him, Pierce wasn't particularly interested in a good impression anymore.

"There's a main dish in the big one," Hal said, smiling. "Probably protein." He sniffed the air.

"Chicken, you think?" Pierce asked, although the smell was a little gamier.

"Turkey?" Hal frowned. "No… but something birdlike. Ain't beef. Anyway, there's a winter salad under the clear dish."

"And we know this because…."

"It's wearing a fur coat," Hal said, smirking.

Pierce grinned, relieved. That was his man. The angry, frustrated kid who'd been trying valiantly to be civil to his mother had borne little resemblance to the confident, perky young man who had won Pierce's heart. "And pearls?"

Hal frowned, squinting into the dish. "Apple slices and mayonnaise, I think."

They both grimaced. "That's awful. Anybody who puts raisins in mayonnaise…."

"Doesn't deserve either raisins or mayonnaise!" Hal supplied, reassuringly outraged. "Gross. Well, we know we don't want salad. What else we got?"

"Harold," Mrs. Lombard hissed. "Put that cover down right now. You know how your father feels about cold food!"

"Well, then he should be downstairs by now," Hal said tightly. "You've both been unconscionably rude to a guest. Now I'm hungry and so is he, and we've got a long drive back. I mean, we're not going to return for years, if ever. We might as well get a bite to eat."

Pierce let some of his insecurity show in his wobbly smile. "You're really going to choose me?" he asked quietly.

"I already have," Hal murmured back. Then he raised his voice again. "So, in this bowl, we've got greens fried with bacon. Here, let me get you some."

"Harold!"

But Hal was on a roll, dishing up greens, potatoes, bread—there was plenty of food at the table, and Pierce really was hungry. And pissed. And hurting for his lover, who hadn't deserved this sort of homecoming and had definitely deserved more than this sort of home.

"So," Pierce said, as Hal reached for the biggest cover, "you ready for the big reveal?"

"Maybe it's something extinct," Hal said, glaring daggers at his mother—who was still standing behind her chair like she was glued there.

"Like your education," Mrs. Lombard shot back. And Pierce felt that remorse again.

"Are you sure you want to leave your education behind?" he asked soberly.

"I'd do it twice. I'd torch my records. I'd go back and take all my massage credits again," Hal vowed, looking intensely into his eyes.

"But I might not be worth it," Pierce said softly.

"Bullshit," Hal told him.

"But—"

"Wabbit season," Hal said unexpectedly.

"What?" Pierce had to laugh.

"Wabbit season!" Hal insisted, the smile crinkles in the corners of his amazing eyes deepening.

"Are we even having a wabbit season discussion?" Pierce wanted to know. This was usually a safe word for them when their discussion got too heavy, too painful.

"Sure we are!" Hal told him, his voice losing the anger, the embarrassment, the tightness of being here with his disapproving mother and a father who couldn't bother to come down for dinner. "I want to tell you all the reasons you're worth it, but I'm damned if I let my mother hear. Wabbit season!"

"I give. Duck season."

Hal grinned and nodded, and suddenly Pierce knew at least one answer they would get about life that night. "Wabbit season," he said soberly.

"Duck season," Pierce argued, and they both grinned evilly. "Want to see?"

"God yes. Wabbit season." He set his hand on the trencher handle.

"Duck season," Pierce said, putting his hand next to Hal's.

"One, two, three," Hal counted.

"*Bang!*" they both chorused, pulling the food cover off on three.

Sure enough, neck stretched out, head intact, was a complete roast duck.

They both burst out laughing.

"Oh my God!" Pierce chortled.

"I can't eat that!" Hal laughed. "I don't know how I ever could."

"That's… oh dear God!"

They were still laughing when Hal stood up and offered Pierce his arm. "Can you make it to the front?" he asked. "I'll have Daniel bring the car around. We can sit on the steps until he gets there."

Pierce nodded, pretty sure he'd crawl through broken glass not to sit at that table for another minute. They made their way, step by step, toward the hallway and actually made it to the front door, where Hal pushed a little red buzzer.

"Yes?" came Daniel's creaky voice.

"Daniel, I'll need my SUV, please."

"So soon, sir?"

"Well, I'm not returning in the near future, so you don't have to worry about that, okay?"

"Yes, sir."

Hal let go of Pierce's waist and grabbed the door handle. "Can you make it through to the steps?"

"Yeah. I'll need your help down," Pierce said, his mortification complete. "It's like the perfect metaphor for me reaching too high for myself."

"Wabbit season," Hal muttered. "All the things I want to say to you about why you're so much better than this place, but I'm not going to do it here."

"Duck season," Pierce conceded. "I'm just so glad you're leaving with me, I'm not even going to argue."

"Harold!" It was a thundering male voice. "Harold Justice Lombard the Fifth—"

"Go, go, go!" Hal shushed. "Let's let him think we're gone."

Pierce should have stayed. He should have been the grown-up. But his body was buckling and he hurt for his lover and all he wanted to do—*all* he wanted to do—was hold the young man whose spirit was so indomitable, it had survived this giant sinkhole of loneliness and pain.

He limped outside with Hal on his heels, and they were both sitting on the white porch steps when the door flew open.

"Hal?"

Hal looked up to the top of the stairs, hurt in his eyes. "Dad?"

"You're not even going to stay for dinner?" The man who stood by the french doors was not tall—but then, neither was Hal. But while Hal was slender and lithe and fit, this man was portly, with jowls and a fireplug body. This was Hal if he ever stopped doing yoga and working out and started eating… well, all the stuff on that table, actually.

"Nope, Dad. Too expensive to eat here."

"Don't be silly, Hal—we don't charge you—"

"My soul. I brought the love of my life home to you and you couldn't even come down on time. Staying here might get me lots more money, but I don't like the cost to my soul."

Hal's father harrumphed. "Why'd you bother to come here at all?"

Pierce grimaced. "My fault, sir," he said. "I thought that maybe Hal's parents would know what an awesome kid they had and would want to wish him well. Even a college graduate can make some piss-stupid mistakes."

"Like spiriting my son away—"

Pierce's eyes never left Hal's. "Like doubting his word for even a moment." He took Hal's hand and kissed his knuckles. "I'll never doubt you again."

Hal's pretty eyes grew shiny. "Duck season," he said, giggling.

"Wabbit season," Pierce told him back.

They both grinned. "Bang," they said in unison.

The car appeared around the corner then, coming slowly as Daniel performed his duties. Hal stood and gave Pierce a hand up. "You and me, Bugs?"

"Sure, Daffy." He made it to the bottom of the stairs and then turned to smile at Hal's father. "Next time, sir, if your son comes to visit, you might want to come out and talk to him. He's a really amazing man."

They both turned, and Hal helped him into the SUV and then gave Daniel a hug—and a tip—and they took off back down the tree-lined drive.

They made plans to stop somewhere and eat on the way to the hotel. They told jokes about cartoons. They sang to some more of Hal's pop music. They talked about going to see baseball and basketball games when they got to Sacramento. They touched hands often.

They never looked back.

CHAPTER 6
DETOURS

THEY STOPPED at an outlet store two days after North Carolina. Pierce said it was getting cold enough that they both deserved something cozy after dealing with Hal's parents, especially as they navigated up north, where winter got fucking real.

"Will it help us deal with the frostbite of visiting my parents?" Hal asked dryly as they both tried on thick coats.

Pierce wrapped a bright fleece scarf around Hal's neck and winked. "You'll have to check my toes tonight to make sure."

"Your toes? Is that a spot I've been neglecting?" Oooh... interesting. Hal had never known a guy with sensitive feet.

Pierce thought about it. "Not that I know of." A dark red crescent formed at each high cheekbone. "I, uh, do like it when you massage my feet and legs, though."

Hal did a little happy dance in the store. "And not just in the 'Oh, thank you, Mr. Professional, I appreciate being pain-free' way, right?"

Pierce snorted and turned toward a row of hats, grabbed a bright orange and purple stocking hat to go with the yellow scarf. "Uh, no. Not in that particular way."

Hal looked at the accessories with raised eyebrows. "Are you trying to tell me I'm gay?"

And those dark red crescents spread all over Pierce's face and neck. "I think we've already established you like men," he said primly. "I was just trying to tell you that you look good in bright colors. And...." Hal could practically feel the heat radiating from his body through the thick wool coat he was trying on. "And I like looking at you in them."

Pierce's flush seemed to be trying to spread to Hal. "Yeah?" he asked, suddenly shy. Would compliments like this ever stop turning his key? "Looking at me in them?"

"Yeah." Pierce nodded, teeth sinking into his lower lip. "Looking at you in them."

"Would you, perhaps, want to look at me out of them?" Hal prompted.

Pierce looked around the public dressing room—deserted in the week after New Year's Day—and shook his head. Not surprising he wouldn't be in for public sex—there was a core of prim conservatism in Pierce. Not the ugly kind that disparaged or shamed, but the quaint kind that kept their relationship personal and private. "Here?"

Hal had to kiss him. "Later," he whispered, taking Pierce's mouth gently.

Pierce gasped, and Hal had to thrust his tongue in, tasting that shyness, that want. Pierce held himself a little aloof—in public, not submitting—but Hal could feel the conflict, the urge to give in, to go for the kiss like it was a world event.

Hal raised his hand to cup Pierce's cheek, and the tag dangling from his coat flapped a little with the movement. Pierce took a deep breath and stepped back. "Later," he promised.

Augh! Hal was erect and aching in his jeans. In college, he and his ex boyfriend would already be giving blowies in the corner and not regret getting kicked out of the store. But Pierce, blushing, shedding the coat into the mesh bag, fumbling for the plain blue scarf he'd picked out to go with it—Pierce would be mortified.

Hal wouldn't change their banter, their playful conversation, their optimism about the future—any of it—for a public blow job. He might be young, but he wasn't stupid. Pierce was worth so much more.

"Not the blue one," he said, voice rough.

Pierce was startled into looking up. "No?"

"It's plain. The light blue one with the red pattern on it. See? Not plain. Not nipple-piercing yellow, but not plain."

Oh, that shy smile would be his undoing. "Okay," he said, and there was Hal's pliant lover, the one who trusted him, even when his body was sore and his heart a little tentative. "We'll take it."

Hal took the bag from him so he could wield his cane, and they grabbed some fleece gloves for Pierce—dark blue—on their way out. After two weeks of dealing with the mild cold of the south, they were ready to deal with the absolute real cold of the East Coast.

They got back into the car again and drove, passing through Maryland and around DC reluctantly.

"I want to see the Natural History museum," Pierce fretted. "I've never been. And the archives and the Capitol—"

"I've seen them," Hal soothed. "But there's a lot of walking. I mean, a lot. You can't just stop and take a cab while you're in the middle of the Air and Space Museum, you know? Maybe we can, you know…." For some reason his heart thundered in his throat. This led to the idea that this road trip—this vacation of sorts—was not the be-all/end-all of their relationship. They'd joked that it was a honeymoon before the wedding—but they weren't planning a wedding, not yet. This was a "Next time we take a bucket list vacation together" sentence, and he hadn't realized it until it snuck up on him and grabbed him by the lapels.

"Next year," Pierce said casually. "It's easier for us to visit Sasha than for her to visit us, right? And I'm making progress by leaps and bounds. Next year I'll be up to more travel. Besides, my house only has two bedrooms—they'd have to stay in a hotel."

Hal swallowed, and that ache in his groin that had never really gone away since the department store renewed again with a vicious throb. This man promised him a home, just that simply. Promised him forever. More trips. More holidays where kids played and hot chocolate was a necessity and people hugged each other after the count of ten. More of Pierce, dryly funny and needy—so needy—but giving that prim little gasp and pulling away because the things Hal wanted to do to his healing body were not meant to be done in public.

Hal would do them in Times Square, but that Pierce wanted those things, just the two of them, together—that was even better.

So, no Smithsonian or Washington Tour for them this trip. Instead they stopped in Delaware, after driving through a heavily wooded section at Pierce's direction. They wound their way to a clearing near a river, where the houses sat maybe every quarter of a mile or so, before pulling up to a two-story clapboard house with red trim and a rainbow of lawn art and wind chimes in the front. Hal got the "go bag," as they'd been calling it—the single small roller board with their shaving kits and pajamas and a single change of clothing in it—and they walked up the stairs to knock on the door together.

The door was thrown open by a middle-aged jovial man with thinning gray hair, skin the color of unbleached linen, and bifocals. "Pierce Atwater?"

Pierce raised his hand. "Yeah, that's us. Jordan Farmer?"

"Yes, sir. You and your fella come on in. Here, young man. Let me get the suitcase—you two got here just in time for dinner. Here—hang up your coats, wash up, and sit down. My wife is serving everybody in the main room."

Jordan disappeared down the hallway, and Pierce and Hal followed, taking his direction to hang up their coats on the pegboard by the door and make a right into the cheery yellow kitchen.

Mrs. Farmer was a perfect counterpoint to her husband—plump, cheery, with graying brown hair pulled back into a ponytail. She smiled at them both, then gestured with her chin because her hands were full with a platter of carved roast. "Go in and wash up, then come sit down. We've got a full house tonight, boys. Let's meet everybody."

Hal found himself smiling back, and Pierce nodded. "Thank you much, ma'am. We'll be right back."

"This is nice," Hal murmured as he soaped up.

"My buddy recced it," Pierce said happily. "Said it was the friendliest B and B he'd ever visited."

"Mm. I don't trust it."

"Don't trust it?" Pierce knit his brows. "What's not to trust?"

"This looks like the family I should have had but got cheated out of. When do they turn to you and ask why you brought your nephew instead of a nice young wife?"

Pierce guffawed. "You know, I booked this place because it was friendly. Maybe I did that for a reason."

Hal closed his eyes and inhaled—roast beef, potatoes, gravy, and some sort of green with cheese on it. "You're trying to fatten me up to eat me?" he hazarded.

Pierce leaned in, an unexpectedly wicked look in his eyes. "Eat dinner with the nice people and behave. The eating will come later."

Hal's mouth dried up, and he almost choked on his tongue. "I hate you. I mean, I love you, but now I gotta go out and talk to strangers and eat roast beast with a woody."

"You can't even *see* if that roast beast has a woody!"

"Augh!"

Pierce's unrepentant chuckle led the way out to the dining room, where an assortment of strangers smiled pleasantly and talked about the historical sights of Pennsylvania and asked which plays they were seeing in New York and generally reaffirmed Hal's faith in mankind again after the awful visit with his parents.

And the roast beast was orgasmically delicious and did nothing to diminish the fierceness of his woody.

By the time they made it past the stairs and to the one bedroom on the ground floor, Hal's stomach was pleasantly sated and his cheeks ached from smiling.

But his want for Pierce hadn't diminished one bit.

He moved just close enough to Pierce to brush his backside with a suggestive hand. "Mm… yes?" he asked, loving that Pierce would get his shorthand.

"Mm… shower. You first," Pierce replied, voice breathy. "I have a plan."

Hal sucked in a breath. "You have a plan?" Hal usually had the plan. He was good at the plan. He was excellent at the plan.

But that didn't mean he didn't look forward to somebody else's plan. To Pierce's plan.

Pierce's heated gaze when he got out of the shower didn't make things any better. Hal grinned and tightened the towel around his waist, feeling heat wash up his neck and across his chest as Pierce grinned back.

"You have a plan," Hal said primly.

"I do."

"Well, remember, whatever your plan is, I might double-go-down on it, so you need to shower too."

Pierce laughed, letting his bathrobe fall as he stepped into the bathroom. "I'll shower, but only just in case."

Hm... just in case? Hal pulled back the decadently fluffy Monet-colored comforter to find the also decadently fluffy mattress covered in sky blue sheets. He spread the towel on the mattress, right dead center, because things might get messy, and then threw himself on the bed facedown and sighed, the rigors of driving not washed away by the shower seeping from his bones.

He might have dozed off a little, because when he came to, Pierce was kissing his way from the back of Hal's knee up his thigh.

"You're going to tickle," Hal mumbled into the marshmallow pillow.

Pierce upped the pressure—but otherwise didn't stray from his course. Hal felt the bed depress behind him and was unsurprised when Pierce nudged his knees apart.

"What're'oo'doooing...," Hal mumbled, drugged by the warmth of Pierce's body between his knees, by the feel of his lips on the soft upper part of his thigh, by the pulsing haze of arousal that had surround him since the store.

"I'm going to tease you," Pierce promised, nuzzling that particularly sensitive spot right below Hal's buttock. He added a little tongue, and the fullness of Hal's erection returned with a vengeance.

"Just teasing?" Hal arched his hips and repositioned his cock, stopping to squeeze and to shiver.

Pierce parted his cheeks and blew slightly into his crease, and Hal's squeeze on his cock turned into a stroke. Hal moaned, and Pierce smacked his bottom. "Stop that!"

"You're taking too long!" Hal complained—but he put both hands up near his head, flat against the mattress.

"Stay right there." The mattress shifted, and for a moment Hal was exposed to the air, tingling with arousal. Another shift and Pierce put a clean sock in Hal's hand. "Hold on to that," Pierce ordered softly. "And tell me no if you don't wanna."

"Don't wanna... nungh!"

Pierce licked boldly up his crease. Hal's cock and balls were aching, and the stimulation in this other erogenous zone set his whole body on fire.

"I always wanna rim—job!"

Pierce did it again, and Hal yanked on the sock between his hands to keep his hips firmly pressed against the bed. "Nungh!"

More licking—specific licking. A tongue concentrating in one sensitive pink space kind of licking. Hal lost himself in it, the tongue, the licking, the lubed finger... "Mmm?"

"Bad?" Pierce asked.

"Good," Hal mumbled. He topped—Pierce. But in his other relationships he... hadn't. This wasn't about who was dominant or who called the shots. This was about... oh God, another finger. Yes!

Pierce pulled both fingers out, and Hal whimpered. "Roll over," Pierce told him. "I have a—"

"You'd better say surprise dick," Hal said excitedly, rolling over carefully so he didn't whack Pierce in the head with his foot.

Pierce rocked back on his knees and laughed throatily, and oh my God, he was naked in the light. A month and a half—really? It had been a month and a half—the thought was staggering—but a month and a half of making love in the dark, because Pierce was ashamed of his body, of his scars, of the muscles that hadn't built back yet, and here he was, naked, a sex flush washing his freckled body from groin to throat, his erection practically purple and shiny to boot.

Hal looked at him, drank him in, so beautiful, and swallowed. "Come here," he whispered, holding out his arms.

"But I was going to—"

"You can top from on top of me while I kiss you. It's why it's called topping."

"I can not," Pierce mumbled, stretching out anyway. Oh God. He could do that. Yes, he'd been in pain on Hal's parents' doorstep, but two days of recovery, of massages, of short drives, and he could move like a man who very much wanted to go body to body with his younger lover, and Hal groaned with the silken luxury of skin on skin.

He couldn't even breathe before he kissed Pierce, their bodies undulating on the plush mattress, Pierce's cock wasted in a pleasant free-for-all around Hal's cock, which actually ached.

Hal's asshole missed the stretch, the burn, and he needed. "Rock back on your knees," he instructed, and Pierce did, carefully but not wincing. "Now—"

Pierce thrust against his ring, breached him. "I know how to fuck," he muttered, thrusting forward slowly.

"Ah! God! You so do!"

Pierce kept pushing forward, more, more, and Hal let out a low moan and a shudder. Ah, God, he loved this. He had forgotten how much he loved this, but… oh yes!

"Good?" Pierce rasped.

"Nungh! Gah! Yes! Don't stop!"

A dreamy smile washed over Pierce's lean features. "Never." He set an easy pace then, not too hard, not too fast, just slow and sure enough to drive Hal out of his everlovin' mind.

"Pierce…." He was pleading. "Can you?"

Pierce shook his head, half regret, half wickedness. "Fast as I can go, baby. You're gonna just have to…."

"Ah! Ah! Ah!" They couldn't yell or shout or scream each other's names—but that quiet privacy Hal had recognized in the changing room, here in a bed, in this fantasy bedroom, became something more potent, something stronger.

Intimacy.

Pierce's body in his was intimate—as so many others had not been. The wickedness gleaming in his eyes was a charm only for Hal. Pierce's smell—soap and Pierce—and his sharp little gasps as he thrust—those were Hal's, made for him as nothing else in a life of monogrammed desk sets and embossed iPhones had been.

And because this moment—Pierce filling him, giving him all the sex his healing body could handle—was only theirs, it was enough. No pounding, no screaming, no raw animal rutting, it was still almost more than Hal could handle. He gasped, sweating, needing, too full of emotion, of sex, of pleasure to bear it.

"Help yourself," Pierce invited, arching his back and sucking in his stomach so Hal could fit his hand in.

But he didn't need to. The change in position, the little ripple of his hips, and…. Hal let out a sobbing breath and climaxed, the orgasm pulled from his body in a haze of pleasure and passion and need.

His come spattered, hot and sticky between them, and Pierce threw his head back, gritting his teeth. Hal kept clenching, still shaking, and that was what Pierce needed to send him over.

Hal could feel him, scalding and vibrant as he pumped inside Pierce's body. The heat of it, the knowledge that this man would be inside him forever, visceral and real, sent Hal into one more spasm.

Pierce groaned and collapsed, still solidly lodged in Hal's ass, and Hal whimpered.

"I hurt you?"

"No. Just… so good."

"Mmm… I may not be able to move tomorrow."

"You'll be great," Hal told him. "God, the way I feel, tomorrow we can fly."

"Course. For you, I'll fly."

Hal chuckled weakly. "You know something?"

"What?" With a grunt and a tiny pain sound Pierce pulled out of him and rolled off, and for a moment they were naked and cooling under the ceiling fan and the heating vent. "Besides me needing help with my shorts."

"In a minute." Hal reached over and traced an invisible line down the curve of Pierce's shoulder, the gentle bulge of his bicep. Even at peak fitness, he'd still be lean. "This is important."

"Hm?" Pierce turned his head, his eyes that clear green/hazel that Hal could only see with the lights on.

"You know how you promised me forever and we both believed it could happen?"

"Yeah?"

"It's more than just belief, you know?"

"What do you mean?" A tiny frown knit between Pierce's brows, and Hal rolled over just to trace it.

"It's like we're already living forever. It's happening every day between us. We've been together six weeks, and it's not nearly enough, but it's a beginning. We've started. I mean, I kept thinking once we got to Sacramento that's when it would start. But we're already a beginning. We're moving to the beginning of the middle, and I can't wait."

Pierce's smile would always have that hint of shyness that made Hal want to squeeze him so tight nothing could hurt him again.

"Don't have to wait. Just kiss me again. We're on our way."

Hal closed his eyes and took his mouth, letting the intimacy flow through him, permeate his bones. This was real. It wasn't "happening," it had "happened," and they would make it continue to happen even after they got to Pierce's home and rediscovered normal in each other's arms.

CHAPTER 7
PRACTICING FOR THE HONEYMOON

NEW YORK was—well, that really felt like a honeymoon.

Pierce was good to walk carefully for a couple of blocks, and they were near the theater district. Three plays in three nights—they didn't get to see *Hamilton*, but *Something Rotten* was a go, and Hal was in heaven.

They ate at a burger place that served duck burgers and buffalo burgers one night, and at an Italian place that served a chicken parmesan to die for the next, and on the day after that, Korean barbecue that Hal would never forget.

On the third day it snowed heavily, so on the fourth day, they took a cab to the Met.

"Really?" Hal asked. "You want to see a museum?"

"You don't?" Pierce sounded stunned, like it was unthinkable that somebody wouldn't want to go see… what? A bunch of old art? But whatever.

"No, no—we did the Statue of Liberty the first day, and the plays have been great! You want to see art, we'll see art." Pierce had sat on a bench in the cold and rested while Hal went to climb inside the statue, but when Hal came back outside, Pierce had such an amazingly serene look on his face. He'd needed to sit in a warm tub for an hour after they got back before he could get dressed for the play, but Hal would have skipped the play just to see the peace in his heart that came from taking Hal somewhere wonderful.

Pierce got a gentle smile on his face in that moment, and for the first time in forever, Hal remembered he was older. "Sure," he said, grabbing Hal's hand and kissing his knuckles. "We'll see art."

Hal bit his lip and looked away. "There's nothing wrong with art," he said, trying to leach the doubt from his voice.

"Of course not," Pierce said mildly before wincing. "Just like there's nothing wrong with coming back a little early, taking a hot shower, watching some television, and—"

"And having hot sex." Hal nodded fervently—he knew how to keep his priorities straight.

"Well, duh." Pierce winked, wrapped a warm scarf around his neck, and grabbed his new thick winter coat.

And the Metropolitan Museum of Art was... well, it was amazingly grand.

The great marble entryway inspired hush and reverence—even with the crowd. And Pierce looked at the exhibits and chose carefully—the Egypt exhibit had to wait; there were stained glass and Impressionist paintings to see.

Together they walked slowly through the stained glass exhibit, where some of the windows were backlit against dark backgrounds so they could be seen as they were meant to be seen.

And oh, the colors were extraordinary, every shape a marvel in precision, every color placement an inspired bit of rainbow magic.

They came to one window, a three-paneled landscape with vines of vinca wrapped around the panel edging and a garden of wildflowers beyond. A sunset peeked through purple clouds, and Hal actually stopped and caught his breath.

"That... that looks like what summer should look like," he said quietly. "Like... like I think of your house, with a pool, and... and looking out your back door, and I know it's stupid, but that's what I think it should be."

Pierce looked stricken. "It's small," he apologized. "But it's going to fit a pool, and there are rosebushes and bougainvillea and marigolds that we pay a gardener to keep. But...." He grimaced. "It's not glorious, you know. It's just...."

But it didn't matter. Something about the colors, the contrast, the beauty so bright it hurt the eye, had already broken Hal's heart and remade it.

"We can buy a print of this?" he asked hopefully.

"I'm sure." It was one of the most prized windows in the collection.

"I want to frame it. Because… because coming home with you, this is what it feels like. Even if it's all weeds and dirt and a giant hole in the ground… this is what the thought of home with you feels like."

Oh fuck.

His eyes weren't just burning. His throat wasn't just swollen. He was crying with the exquisiteness of the dream.

But Pierce didn't seem to mind. People streamed around them, but Pierce stopped and pulled the sleeve of his sweater over his palm so he could wipe Hal's cheeks.

"It's a map," he said, his own eyes shiny.

"A map?" Hal asked, his throat still thick.

"You know, people only get perfection in art, right? But it's like… like a map to the soul. We'll get the print, and this can be our map. This is what we'll want our life to look like. And even if we get it wrong sometimes, and the pool gets shitty and the flowers die, we know that when we look in our hearts, we want this, and we'll work to make it happen."

Hal smiled through the stupid emotional tears that were starting to piss him off. "That's how unicorns work," he said soberly.

A tear tracked down Pierce's cheek, but he nodded anyway. "And that's us, right?"

"Yeah."

Pierce kissed him then, their breath mingling with salt, and then he pulled away. "You ready to keep going?" he asked after a moment.

Hal nodded, remembering that night at the bed and breakfast. "I'm really ready for the beginning of the middle," he said soberly.

Pierce bit his lip. "Well, you know, we were going to go north and see all the stuff up there, but you know something?"

Hal half laughed. He'd seen the weather reports too. "It's fucking January?" he said.

"Yeah. One more day in New York to sleep, and let's just go home."

Hal's heart suddenly opened up to that stained-glass vista. "So, like, we can be…." And the word caught in his throat, because he realized, right then in front of that image of unachievable perfection, that this thing in this window was a thing he'd never had. "We can be home?"

"Five days, balls-out," Pierce confirmed.

Hal threw his arms around him, holding him tight and shaking. "Being home with you is better than this picture," he said.

"You haven't heard me whine after five days of balls-out driving," Pierce gasped, but he didn't struggle out of Hal's embrace. They needed it too much, needed the contact, the promise, the affirmation of all the things they'd said on Christmas Eve—almost four weeks before.

"I'll take anything you can dish out," Hal promised—mostly because Pierce's shitty moods were never as bad as advertised, but also because he could. He could be strong when Pierce needed it.

In moments just like this one, Pierce could be absolutely everything Hal needed.

"Good." Pierce went limp in his arms, in a way he hadn't that day in the dressing room. "I want you home more than anything."

Another breath. Another heartbeat. Another moment drawing strength from each other and they drew apart. Logically they were headed for the food court for lunch, and then to see the Impressionists. But as they turned their back on that perfect view of the world for the admittedly imperfect world of their own hearts, they knew they were really taking their first real steps home.

CHAPTER 8
ON THE WAY HOME

YOU HAD to drive carefully in the snow. You didn't make a lot of time, and stopping to rest frequently became their watchword.

Hal spent a lot of moments with his face pressed up against the glass, his fingers white-knuckled around the steering wheel, cursing silently to himself with the background noise of 90s music that Pierce kept on the radio.

He was particularly a fan of Nirvana and Pearl Jam. Go figure.

After a quick trip to Pennsylvania because neither of them had seen the Liberty Bell or Independence Hall, it was, as Pierce had promised, pretty much balls-out driving.

On day two, Pierce asked if it would bother Hal if he broke out his tablet so he could do some work for the job waiting for him in March, and Hal had to ask, "You're not going to turn into a closet workaholic on me, are you?"

Pierce grunted. "I hope not." Hal heard him take a deep breath. "Not like your father, I promise."

"Well, that is sort of a low bar." Hal's parents had been hideous to Pierce—Hal hated to think Pierce was anything like them.

"I worked a lot with Cynthia in the end," Pierce confessed. "I... you know. Didn't like going home. But this is just email and employee application stuff. I... I promised you a home. Stability. A pool—"

"The pool is optional!" Hal gasped, because he hated to think of it as a burden.

"Yeah, I know. But part of that promise is me bringing in money. You know. Being productive. I mean, you'll probably pay your share of the bills whether I ask you or not, but I just want to... you know. Be dependable for you." Pierce let out a sort of humorless grunt. "It's not like I can promise excitement or glamour. If dependability is what I've got, I'm going to run with it."

"Dependability is not why I fell in love with you," Hal told him, although maybe it was and Hal just hadn't thought of it like that.

"I'm still fuzzy on what it was that actually made you do that." Pierce tapped on his tablet fitfully, staring at his email like it had offended him. "Enlighten me."

"You smelled good."

Pierce smirked. "I smelled like Bengay."

"No—you should have smelled like Bengay, but God forbid you actually use any painkillers. No, you just smelled like... you know. Redheaded sweat and chlorine. But it was a good smell on you. I could smell it every day."

"Well, I'll be sure to wave my pit-stink at the bank when we drive by, and maybe it will fill up my coffers," Pierce said dryly— although Hal knew he was in pretty good shape, all things considered.

"Well, they do call it filthy lucre." Hal guffawed, and he liked Pierce's answering laugh, but the thought still bothered him.

Apparently it still bothered Pierce as well.

"I like work," Pierce said unexpectedly after a few moments of driving. "I like feeling useful, feeling smart. I'm designing video chips for a new game company—it's fun. It's like tiny changes in my work can make people really happy in their play. Why not like that? I mean, it's not turning someone from a cramped pain ball into an actual human being like some of us can do, but it's not bad."

"So the workaholic thing?" Hal prompted, actually liking this answer better than a flat-out no.

"Probably not a problem. I may have to work some project deadlines, but I got to tell you, if home is a good place to be, I really love my weekends and my afternoons. Derek and I usually play softball in the spring—"

"I love softball!" Hal exclaimed, delighted. Oh, this was unexpected. "I also play rec-league soccer—"

"We've got some indoor leagues around," Pierce told him, and he almost shuddered in happiness. "And trips to the river and car shows and—you know. Fun. I'm a fan. So I don't think there'll be a lot of late nights, you know? Where I'm not there. Just... I guess you were wondering."

Hal half laughed. "You know, the thing we didn't really think about before we rode into the sunset was that we'd have time to plan what the sunset would look like. I'm thinking this could be a real fuckin' gorgeous sunset, right?"

"It's looking good so far!"

The next night—coming through Oklahoma, of all places— it wasn't quite so golden. Pierce's legs cramped up about halfway through their drive, leaving Hal to find an off-ramp so he could hurriedly work out the worst of the spasms. But three days of driving had taken its toll, and Hal pulled out the emergency pain meds, the ones Pierce kept tucked in his big suitcase that he tried not to take too many of, just so Pierce's muscles could relax enough for Hal to stretch them out. Pierce was left limp, more than a little stoned, sweating in the chill of the winter air, and wrung out in the passenger seat of Hal's CR-V.

"We need a bed," Hal said, no bullshit in his voice. "And a pool. And it's got to be a good one—no Motel 6, okay?"

"I've got some websites on my phone." Pierce yawned, because pain could sap a man's energy like nothing else, and Hal pulled the phone out of his fingers before he could start tapping.

"Let me, okay? The closest good hotel, I promise."

"I won't always be helpless," Pierce mumbled. "I swear."

"Oh, baby." Hal put a warm hand on the part of his back that had been spasming the hardest. "I'm not ever worried about you being helpless. I'm worried about you trying to do this alone, you get that, right?"

"I'd miss you," Pierce mumbled. "Being alone sucked."

"You are telling me. Okay...."

"Hey, queers, get a room!"

Hal looked up from his fumbling with the phone and realized they were at a truck stop in Oklahoma and he was actively fondling his boyfriend. He glared at the guy who had just spoken—his age, but with the sagging skin of poor nutrition and too much tobacco.

"I'm looking for a good one," Hal told him shortly. "Somewhere that wouldn't take you, for instance."

Next to him, Pierce chuckled. "You are going to get us killed, but at least I'm too high to care."

"Close your door, baby," Hal muttered, shifting the phone in his hand so he could do the same. The big country boy who liked to catcall got there before he could, though.

"What'samatter? He sick?"

Hal glared at him sourly. Hair so blond it was white completed the picture of redneck. "He's recovering from a car accident. We just need a place for him to lie down and stretch out."

"Well, hell—you can do that at my place—it's not that far down the road." The guy repositioned the John Deere hat on his head, and Hal blessed and cursed Southern hospitality.

"That's kind," he said frankly, "but since we really are queer, I'm not sure how much you mean that. We've got a hotel about twenty miles away—I think we'll try to get there."

"Why're you queer?" the kid said, and Hal heard Pierce's dry snort next to him.

"That's just who we are," Hal told him. "Thank you for asking—"

"No, seriously. You can come to my house—if he's sore, it's right there—you can see it. Here, I'll drive, you follow."

And before Hal could protest again, the kid got into his truck and started it up, checking his mirrors and nodding to make sure Hal would follow him.

"Now would be a great time to drive the hell away," Pierce mumbled.

Hal hesitated before putting the SUV into gear. "No, seriously. I think he's being kind. And if I could work on you for an hour some place you could stretch out, we might be able to make it to Oklahoma City, which could have a hotel with a Jacuzzi."

"You sure he doesn't think you have a purty mouth?" Pierce asked.

"No, Pierce, that's you." Hal took a deep breath and decided to follow the kid with the white hair. "I'm going to take a gamble, okay? If we both die horribly, don't hate."

"I promise," Pierce mumbled. "Not hating."

"Good."

Well, if they were going to be unicorns, they might as well throw themselves into danger, right?

The kid wasn't kidding—his house was about a quarter of a mile from the truck stop, back from the road a little with a long driveway, but not deep into the swamp either.

"I could be just getting desperate here, but that place doesn't look half-bad."

Pierce hit the lever on his side of the car and levitated slowly up. The house was two stories and in decent repair. The kudzu that dominated the topography had been pruned back to leave about an acre's worth of bluegrass lawn, complete with a modest flower garden in front of the porch. It wasn't Hal's parents' house by any means, but it wasn't a shack in the middle of nowhere either.

"The flower beds don't even look big enough for a human body," Pierce said in wonder, and Hal smirked.

At that moment, the white-haired kid hopped out of the pickup truck and went thundering into the house. "Aunt Lucy! Aunt Lucy! We got queers here who need fixing! Aunt Lucy!"

"They're going to try to pray the gay away, aren't they?" Hal asked in numb horror.

"Yup. Got your gay held tight in both hands?"

Hal glared at him. "How about you—got your bi in one hand and your sex in the other?"

Pierce managed a rusty chuckle before closing his eyes and consciously relaxing. God, Hal hoped this wasn't a bad idea, because pretty much every muscle in Pierce's body had decided that travel was the suck.

The woman who came running down the porch was something of a surprise.

She was not, all told, much older than Pierce himself, with a few streaks of gray in her shoulder-length brown bob. She was wearing faded mom jeans over a waifish figure and an oversized sweatshirt with Don't Hate on the front in rainbow letters.

Hal felt a knot in the middle of his back start to loosen up. If he was not mistaken, they had managed to find themselves a blue liberal in the middle of a red state. They might not get buried in the flower beds after all.

He hopped out and went to shake her hand.

"See, Aunt Lucy—I told you, we got queers who need fixing!"

Aunt Lucy cast a pained look at her nephew. "Kyle?" she said gently. "Does it matter if they're queer?"

"Well, yeah, because they were in the middle of the truck stop, and they were gonna get clobbered. I told them to get a room, but this one said his boyfriend was hurt."

"Hurt?" Lucy had big brown compassionate eyes. "Does he need a doctor?"

Hal shook his head. "He just needs to not be in the car for an hour, someplace he can stretch out. He's recovering from some injuries and he's getting better, but we were trying to get to California in another three days."

"Mm," she said, shaking her head and going over to Pierce's side of the car. "Overdid it. I hear you. What's in California?"

Hal opened the door for Pierce and offered his arm so Pierce could grab hold. "Home," he said quietly. "We were vacationing in Florida, and we met, and… well, I'm going home with him."

The woman's quiet smile sort of lit up the gray winter day. "That's lovely," she said. "That's damned near the most romantic thing I've ever heard. Here, uh—"

"Pierce," Pierce supplied. "Ma'am, I don't want to squash you."

Aunt Lucy was about five three.

"You're right. Kyle, get in there, you and—"

"Hal."

"Hal, pleased to meet you. You two make a little sedan chair and take Pierce to the downstairs guest bedroom. It's all made up and everything. You can stretch out there. Do you need any painkillers?"

"I'm on some," Pierce said dryly. "Not as much fun as they could be."

Lucy chuckled. "Well, we'll try to change that. I've got some really awesome menthol ointment in my medicine chest—do you think that would work?"

"Lady, you're a godsend," Hal breathed, taking Pierce's weight without trouble as Kyle did the same thing on his other side. "I'm a massage therapist—if I can just work out his muscles for an hour or so, we can get out of your hair."

"No worries—and no hurries either. The roads get icy at night, and I just made a big helping of venison stew."

"Hunting's been good this year," Kyle said proudly, and Hal couldn't even make fun of that. His parents served a full-sized duck, head and everything, at their dinner table, just to prove they could. Apparently these people ate deer because they could shoot their own, and that was actually better.

"It's nice of you to offer," Hal said humbly. "Let's see how he's doing first. We really did want to get home."

Lucy's pat on his arm was reassuring. "A little detour here and there won't hurt too bad. Your lives together will start soon enough. Now let me go first and strip the bed and put down an old sheet—you can get ointment all over it and not worry."

They got Pierce to the bed, and Hal stripped him down to his T-shirt and boxer shorts out of deference to Lucy and Kyle. She brought in a big brown jar of something Hal tried not to grimace at. Lucy was pretty sharp, though, because she laughed.

"I know—you're thinking hillbilly witchcraft, right?"

He smiled and tried for diplomacy. "It's not, uh, from the catalog I usually use."

Her laugh turned to a cackle. "You are sweet. Trust me. It's eucalyptus and lavender and chamomile and willow bark. All stuff that will seep into his muscles and take away the pain. Except the lavender—that's just for the smell. And it's water-based—it'll wash off just fine. Now go ahead, rub it on him. Is it okay if I watch? I got training myself, and I might pick up a few things."

Hal nodded. "Okay, Pierce? She wants to watch."

"I'd say that was kinky, but I don't even know her."

Lucy laughed again. "Oh, he's salty. You two must be a laugh riot. Now here's some gloves for you." she produced two nonlatex gloves, the type used by most doctors, and Hal nodded thanks again before putting them on, getting a dab of the salve, and trying it on his own shoulder.

He gave a little sigh as the salve went hot and cold on his skin, and he figured it would be just like Icy Hot or Aspercreme, but it smelled a hell of a lot better.

"If this is a bad move, start screaming," he muttered to Pierce.

Pierce, stretched out on the bed and completely immobile, only grunted. "Sure. Screaming. I'll get right on that."

Hal rubbed at the base of Pierce's spine, and the whimper he let out sounded nothing like screaming at all.

An hour later, Hal's back and shoulders were aching from exertion but Pierce was finally asleep.

"Gah!" he breathed, lifting his arms up in stretches. "That was bad. He didn't say anything this morning when we got up to leave—"

"He wants to be home as bad as you do," Lucy supplied. "Now here. I'm not getting fresh or anything, but take off your sweatshirt and let me rub your back and arms through your shirt. You've earned some care of your own."

Hal couldn't object, and he sat down in the chair she'd used when he'd been working. "That's really kind," he said, relaxing his head on his neck. "Pierce is usually a pretty good caretaker. Makes sure I get some food, makes sure I'm okay inside. This... this isn't going to last."

Her hands felt wonderful—sexless but wonderful—on his neck, his shoulders, his back.

"The pain won't," Lucy told him, "but I think the love will. Anyone that salty when he's in that much pain isn't going to let a few bumps in the road get him down."

Hal half laughed. "He was afraid at first—he'd be too... well, salty, I guess you'd say. But that's not really the case, you know?"

"I can see. You want some of that salve on your neck here? You've got a nasty knot. You've been doing all the driving, right?"

Hal moaned softly. "You're not going to kill us while we sleep and bury us in the flower beds, are you?"

"No, son—we were going to cook you up as barbecue, but the salve gives the meat a funny taste, so we may just have to feed you and let you go."

Hal laughed and pulled off his shirt. "Talk about salty!"

"Yeah, yeah—let's just say I'm waiting for a smartass of my own, but they don't come to this part of the world often." She rubbed some of the ointment into his back with effort, and the relief in his muscles was so acute, the long-term headache he'd been ignoring for two days disappeared. "And when they do," she added, working at the base of his skull with her fingers, "they're not my type."

Hal felt drugged. "Sorry about the queer," he mumbled, close to just passing out next to Pierce.

"Don't be. The queer is fine—it's the male I've got a problem with. If you could send, maybe, a pretty little homebody back from California who wants an Oklahoma gal, I'd be much obliged."

That did it. Hal started to chuckle, eyes half-lidded, as he fought falling asleep in the chair.

"Done," Lucy said gently. "Go lie next to your young man. I'll have dinner for you both in an hour, then you can do some walking around the yard before bedtime. You'll both be better for it in the morning, and Kyle can learn to talk to you without thinking 'queer queer queer' the whole time. It's really the one lesson I haven't been able to pound into his head."

"He's kind, though," Hal murmured, standing up and lying down on the empty side of the bed. "He get that from you?"

"Well, certainly not from my brother, who was an asshole, or from his mother, who was just not that bright. But they're off, making more babies somewhere else, and I got a chance to fix this one."

"He offered us shelter when we needed it," Hal told her, because this was important. Lucy got what was apparently an old blanket from a closet in the room and shook it out over the two of them. "I mean, kindness of strangers—this has been almost like… a gift. A wedding present from the gods." He pulled a corner of the blanket around his shoulder and snuggled down. Lucy patted his arm.

"Well, maybe the gods give you nice things because you're so sweet about accepting them," she said. "I'll wake you for dinner, okay?"

"Thank you."

"Sleep tight."

She left, turning off the light and closing the door, and Pierce made a sound next to him, rolling over to his side.

"You okay?" Hal asked, anxiety pulling him awake a little.

"I can move. It's a miracle. Come here closer—we both smell, and it feels like we should smell together."

Hal chuckled and curled into his chest. "They're not even going to chop us up for barbecue," he said, still stunned at their good fortune.

"Now see, if it had been me alone, I'd be in the oven already, slow cooking," Pierce said soberly. "It's all you, baby. I'm sure of it."

"Mm…." Hal snuggled harder. "It's us. We're unicorns. We can find magic people. It's a superpower."

"Anybody else, I'd think that was bullshit," Pierce said, and on that note they fell asleep.

They woke up later in the evening and broke bread with Lucy and Kyle, then took a walk with their dogs before coming back to sleep. In the morning, Hal cooked omelets for everybody to say thank you, and then they were on their way, with homemade cornbread wrapped in a towel to eat for lunch.

And Pierce would always assert that it was Hal's magic that found the nice people in Oklahoma, but Hal knew the truth.

It was both of them. They were unicorns.

He couldn't wait to get home to Sacramento, where they could fill Pierce's house with magic!

CHAPTER 9
COMING HOME

THE ABSENCE of snow had made the last three days of driving much easier. Hal had made good time after Oklahoma and through Texas, and he'd managed to stop at some nice hotels in between, so Pierce was in pretty good shape as they pulled off Highway 80 and negotiated their way through a series of surface streets and small suburbs.

"Historic Fair Oaks?" Hal asked, squinting in the dark. It was eight o'clock at night, and Hal was cooked and done. He'd thought he could maintain enthusiasm about anything forever, but the last week of driving had burned him to the bone.

"It looks more historic in the light. Turn right here," Pierce said, eagerness tinting his voice. "And slow, or you'll miss Toyon. Okay— there. Turn right. And left. And… right. Into that driveway there."

Hal's first thought was that Pierce hadn't been kidding when he'd said the place was "little"—but then, Hal had realized that a lot of the land plots in California were smaller than they were in Florida or even in the other states they'd driven through.

These houses, off the road, often hidden in driveway dips or up hills behind heavy foliage, weren't mansions, and Pierce's was no exception. Hal parked in the carport, noting there were no other cars there at all.

"It's weird that you don't have a car," he said bluntly, yawning and stretching as he turned off the ignition.

"Well, my last car was the truck I wrecked," Pierce admitted, looking at the house in the thin winter light. "It's weird how familiar it looks, when my whole life changed."

Hal tried to look at the place objectively after fantasizing about it for nearly two months. It was small—Pierce said three bedrooms— but the siding was a dark blue that wasn't your everyday sort of color, even in the moonlight. The trim was white, and bougainvillea grew over the porch railing and around the support posts, giving it the feeling of being a secret cottage, hidden in lush vegetation.

"There's a door from the carport," Pierce said, sounding as uncertain as Hal felt. "Let's just get the luggage inside and see what we're dealing with bedwise." He paused, smiling slightly. "Think—we can sleep as long as I can manage it tomorrow. And we have no place to go forever."

Hal giggled, a little hysterically. "I can stay here forever. That's not a hardship. Lead the way, O captain—I'll get the roller bags."

Pierce took his time, getting out of the car slowly and stretching in the chill air. Of course, after the East Coast, it was practically balmy—but after Florida, it was frigid. Hal decided he liked the way the weather sort of sat in the middle, and proceeded to drag all their luggage out while Pierce pulled his keys from his pocket and opened the door.

Lights came on inside the house, and Hal heard Pierce's excited exclamation as he rolled the first two bags in.

"Oh wow! Cynthia totally came through!"

"'Cause that's what I want to hear when we arrive," Hal muttered to himself, and then walked into the bedroom and totally took back every mean thought he'd ever had about Pierce's ex. "New bed?" he asked, feeling dumb.

"New bed," Pierce said, sitting on top of the king-sized sleigh-style bed and bouncing. "And it's—" He yawned. "Perfect."

It was already made—probably in the last week—with mint green sheets and a dark green comforter. The frame was sturdy oak, and Hal could tell from Pierce's delight that the mattress was bouncy as hell.

"Get ready for bed, then," Hal told him, some of the anticlimax easing up.

He went out to the car and gathered the rest of the bags, and when he got back, Pierce was standing in front of the bed in his boxers, going through the stretching regime Hal had taught him before they'd left.

Hal stood for a moment and watched him finish, every muscle in his body straining, a look of intense concentration on his face.

"You've gotten so much better at that," Hal said, feeling dreamy and exhausted and odd.

Pierce looked up from a particularly painful stretch and smiled. "I've had good incentive."

Hal smiled a little, realizing he couldn't feel his face, he was so numb from exhaustion. Pierce dropped his stretch and walked over to him, wrapped his arms around Hal's waist, and touched their foreheads.

"Go shower," he said softly. "There's shampoo and soap in the cupboard, and extra toothbrushes and everything. I'll turn on the heater and check out the houseplants and turn on the Wi-Fi. You're done. I can tell. Shower, drop into bed, stay as long as you need to. Eventually you'll stop seeing the road behind your eyes when you close them."

"You see it too?" Hal said plaintively, because it had been on autoloop for the last five days.

"Only every minute of the day. I hope you're done with traveling for a while. I want to stay here, build a pool, and show you the wonder and delight of my tiny corner of the state."

Hal breathed out a sigh of relief. "We have to visit your sister next year," he said, and something about the last two months made that possible. Next year, the two of them at Sasha and Marshall's. It was a date.

"And I really want to go to Europe on our honeymoon," Pierce mumbled dreamily. "Our real honeymoon. When there's rings and a ceremony and everything."

Hal's dizziness grew a little more acute. "Is that a proposal?"

Pierce nuzzled his cheek. "It's an expected outcome. A logical conclusion. I'm so tired I can barely see, and you're going to fall down any second. But I love you more now than I've loved anyone in my life. There has to be a wedding and a marriage. You… you belong here, in this room. Give it a week, a month—I'll ask you then, okay? When we're not hearing the car in every heartbeat and you know the way to the bathroom—"

"Yes," Hal mumbled. "I'd marry you tomorrow. I'll marry you in my sleep. I don't need a week. I mean, I'm gonna need a week— mint green? Was that her choice or yours?"

"Mine," Pierce told him, smiling a little. "I was a redheaded kid—"

"You're a redheaded adult. Whoever told you you weren't was full of shit. But fine. I can live with mint green. As soon as I can see my phone—"

"And it's charged," Pierce said, his smile growing. The phone had died coming through Bakersfield, of all places.

"Yeah, that. I'm gonna buy us a big unicorn pillow pet. And two rings. And every day until we get married we'll walk in through the bedroom door and see the big unicorn pillow pet and the rings. And we'll be just as married the day before the wedding as we will be the day after."

"As we are now," Pierce said happily.

"I so belong here," Hal told him, not even needing to see the backyard. "I so belong here with you."

"God, you do." Pierce's voice grew a little choked, and Hal felt tears starting in his eyes, but their hug wasn't going away.

"I'll shower in a minute," Hal said thickly.

"Yeah."

"I love you so much."

"I love you too."

EVENTUALLY THEY both made it to the shower, and Pierce wandered around the house checking rooms and turning on lights and the Wi-Fi. He sorted the mail on the table and saw the envelope immediately. Big and legal and official-looking. He opened it up and smiled a little, none of the bitterness he'd expected in this moment washing over him, all the sweetness of that mangled proposal filling his heart instead.

Good. That chapter with his wife was closed, and they could move on.

He wandered back to the bedroom, feeling so much better in body and spirit than he had when he'd left Sacramento in November. His body might not ever be back to where it had been before the accident—but his spirit was so much better.

His spirit had found hope. Had found sweetness.

Had found Harold Justice Lombard the Fifth and the joy of being a unicorn.

He crawled into bed and sighed, the sound of Hal's SUV on the tarmac fading from memory.

"Anything interesting?" Hal mumbled.

"Yeah. My divorce will be final in June."

"Good."

"Wanna get married in July?"

"God, yes. Where do you want to honeymoon?"

"Somewhere we can fly."

Hal chuckled. "I love you. Tomorrow we'll see about the pool."

"I love you back. Tomorrow we'll have sex."

"Let's do that first."

"Absolutely. G'night, Hal."

"Mm."

So much to do. So much to see. So much to *live*, all with the man by his side.